KIM JONG FUN

PARTY HARD THE NORTH KOREAN WAY

By Splendid and Incorruptible Comrade

KIM JONG UN

Shining Sun of the Revolution
and Fount of All Our Joy
(Who's Surprisingly Tall, By the Way)

N.B. This book is subject to copyright in
the Democratic People's Republic of Korea.
Any unauthorised use will be met with a lawsuit
or nuclear warhead, whichever is more devastating.

Praise for *Kim Jong FUN*

'All readers must recognise *Kim Jong FUN* as an earth-shattering masterpiece and magnum opus tour de force. The epochal wisdom of our beneficent leader makes the works of Confucius and Aristotle seem like a tramp's deranged rambling. Enemies of our glorious revolution will tremble at Comrade Kim's advice on canapés and doily placement.'

Rodong Sinmun, official newspaper of the Central Committee of the Workers' Party of Korea

'I don't read books, but if I did I'd read this one. Mr Jong Un is a smart cookie, very tough. Unless he says anything bad about me, in which case he's a loser and a moron. Be careful, Little Rocket Man!'

Donald J. Trump,
star of *Home Alone 2: Lost in New York*

'Bloody hell!'

The Ghost of George Orwell

About the Author

Respected Comrade Kim Jong Un has been Supreme Leader of the Democratic People's Republic of Korea since 2011, when state media announced him as 'the Great Successor'. He rose to this position despite humble origins as the son of North Korea's ruler, Kim Jong Il, and the grandson of its founder, Kim Il Sung. A leading Marxist theoretician and maker of five-year plans, he is admired by all for his sage governance and feats of physical strength.

Kim lives in the Ryongsong Residence in north-east Pyongyang, with his wife Ri Sol-ju and an unconfirmed number of children. His hobbies include advancing the people's prosperity, bringing US imperialists to heel and Boggle. He has written over a hundred books and is best known in the West for dating Angelina Jolie from 2007 to 2008.

Also by the Author

*The Jong Un Short of It:
Scenes from a Korean Childhood*

12,892 Rules for Life

How to Kill Friends and Subjugate People

The Da Kimchi Code: Kim's Korean Cookbook

My Family and Other Enemies

The 7 Habits of Highly Oppressive People

*Juche Workout:
A Body Like Mine in Five Easy Steps*

Being a Genius for Dummies

*Mao Money, Mao Problems:
Get Rich the Communist Way*

RIP in the DMZ – A Detective Kim Mystery

The Erotic Adventures of Kim Jong Hung

*The Communist Manifesto 2:
Electric Boogaloo*

KIM JONG FUN

PARTY HARD
THE NORTH KOREAN WAY

This book has not been authorised, licensed or endorsed by Kim Jong Un.

Copyright © Soo Do Nam 2024

The right of Soo Do Nam to be identified as the Author of the Work has been asserted by him in accordance with the Copyright, Designs and Patents Act 1988.

First published in 2024 by Wildfire
An imprint of Headline Publishing Group

1

Apart from any use permitted under UK copyright law, this publication may only be reproduced, stored, or transmitted, in any form, or by any means, with prior permission in writing of the publishers or, in the case of reprographic production, in accordance with the terms of licences issued by the Copyright Licensing Agency.

Cataloguing in Publication Data is available from the British Library.

Hardback ISBN 978 1 0354 2528 0
ebook ISBN 978 1 0354 2529 7

Illustration on p.33 © Shutterstock.com

Designed and set by EM&EN
Printed and bound in Great Britain by Clays Ltd, Elcograf S.p.A.

Headline's policy is to use papers that are natural, renewable and recyclable products and made from wood grown in well-managed forests and other controlled sources. The logging and manufacturing processes are expected to conform to the environmental regulations of the country of origin.

HEADLINE PUBLISHING GROUP
An Hachette UK Company
Carmelite House
50 Victoria Embankment
London EC4Y 0DZ

www.headline.co.uk
www.hachette.co.uk

Legal Note

By reading these words, you have pledged undying fealty to Marshal Kim Jong Un, as well as any descendant of the sacred Mount Paektu bloodline, now and in perpetuity. Should the reader break said pledge, they shall be sentenced to hard labour, execution or the punishment of their family for three generations.

Additionally, all North Koreans must memorise this book in its entirety. The leader of their neighbourhood watch could issue them with a page number at any time. If they are not word perfect in reciting it, they're off to the gulag.

Anyway, enjoy!

THE PARTY IS GOD! DEFEND GOOD VIBES TO THE DEATH!

Note from Translator

It has been the honour of my life to render Heroic Ruler Kim Jong Un's words in English. Though I could never match his scintillating prose, I hope his intellect shines through nonetheless. The honour is doubly meaningful, given my status as a wretched Westerner. (I was prompted to learn Korean by a love of Park Chan-wook's *Oldboy* and the K-Pop girl group Twice.) Despite this deficiency, the Thrice-blessed Chairman of the National Defence Commission saw fit to hire me.

A few months ago, I woke in bed and, as is my wont, grabbed my phone for an hour or so of doomscrolling. That particular morning, I saw a fateful notification, an email from one kimfan69420@propaganda.gov. It read:

> Greetings from best world country North Korea. You receive number-one blessing of serve adored leader Kim Jong Un. Must translate excellent party-planning guide into

ugly Western tongue of English. Answer immediate!

A couple of things occurred to me on reading this. Firstly, that kimfan had almost certainly put his or her message through Google Translate. Secondly, that the North Koreans must have gone quite far down their list of potential translators. Nevertheless, I was intrigued. I called the attached number, with its exotic +850 area code, and was answered before the second ring. A scrupulously polite – if somewhat stern – woman explained the terms of the deal. Should I accept this assignment, I would be expected to travel to the DPRK and work with Kim himself to adapt his book into English.

So that was the offer: spend six weeks in a country Amnesty International considers to be in a category of its own when it comes to human rights violations. I must confess to some trepidation. It was partly the responsibility of conveying the great leader's thoughts. And partly because the previous five translators had mysteriously died.* On top of this, the fee was

---

* That's what I call a ghostwriter! – KJU

surprising low for a project by a world leader. Still, I'm an author with rent to pay – what was I going to do, say no? The gig seemed more interesting – and less of a moral compromise – than copywriting.

The next day I flew from London Heathrow to Hong Kong and then Beijing, before finally landing in Pyongyang. I stepped off my Soviet-made Air Koryo plane and was greeted on the tarmac by a cadre of stone-faced soldiers. They led me, jet-lagged and anxious, to a military vehicle, which drove from the airport to Supreme Leader Kim's compound. Due to Western imperialist brainwashing, I was under the misguided impression that North Korea was a Kafkaesque nightmare in which the value of human life was close to nil. Would I be held hostage, sent to a concentration camp or stripped naked and fed to starving dogs?

Fortunately, none of these fevered imaginings came true. Far from a capricious murderer of family members, Marshal Kim turns out to be a thoroughly chill dude. He is a joy to collaborate with, and I have received unfailing generosity from my communist hosts. At no point have I been forcefully reminded that North Koreans take the word 'deadline' literally. At no point has a Glock been pressed to my temple in a bid to increase word count. And at no point was I injected with a powerful sedative, bundled into a van with tinted windows and deposited in a concrete cell with nothing but a waste bucket and a Soviet-era typewriter.

Yes, this experience has been a dream from start to finish. I have zero complaints about sleep deprivation, the quantity and quality of food or the number of times electrodes have been attached to my genitals. 'Help! Oh God, someone please help!' is precisely the sort of thing you would never hear me say, because, as far as I'm concerned, everything is fine and dandy.

So enjoy this unique and transcendent book.
Appreciate the knowledge in every clause.
Vow to host gatherings worthy of its tuition.
Embrace the Juche method of party-planning.

Many thanks to the regime that made this book happen.
Especially treasured leader Kim Jong Un.

Unnamed translator
Undisclosed location, DPRK
2024

Contents

Introduction xix

Acknowledgements xxix

Dedication xxxi

Denunciation xxxiii

Part One: Diligent Preparation of Exemplary Party According to Socialist Principles

Preliminaries 3

Setting 21

Fashion 30

Part Two: Ruthless Enforcement of Guests' Pleasure During First-Rate Party

Refreshments 43

Entertainment 58

Kim's Film Recommendations 70

Rules 75

Part Three: Further Insights from Remarkable Genius Kim Jong Un

Social Tips 87

Aftermath 100

State-Sanctioned Limericks to be Recited at Party 106

Memories 109

Conclusion 119

Excellent Movie Script by Kim Jong Un 123

Supplementary Dedication 139

INTRODUCTION BY THE PEERLESSLY GREAT AND UNIVERSALLY BELOVED COMRADE-GENERAL KIM JONG UN, WHO IS SO CONCERNED WITH HIS PEOPLE'S WELL-BEING AND THE NATION'S MILITARY MIGHT

Annyeonghaseyo!

It's me. The big boy. Numero Un-o. The Pyongyang Pussy Magnet. And I'm thrilled to introduce this book, which showcases a Kim the world rarely sees.

Look, I have a lot of honorary titles. Invincible and Triumphant General. Guardian of Justice. Best Incarnation of Love. Decisive and Magnanimous Leader. Bright Sun of the Twenty-First Century. But one you might not be familiar with is 'Ultimate Partymeister'. That's a shame, because while I'm an expert on many topics – military strategy, nuclear physics, having a normal haircut – my chief area of expertise is party-planning.

I've loved parties since my fifth birthday, when Dad threw me a lavish bash featuring caterers, magicians and clowns kidnapped from Japan.* Nowadays I'm the archetypical 'big fat party animal', hosting at least 150 parties per year. That might sound a lot, but it really isn't when you consider how many reasons there are to celebrate me. Plus, as Supreme Leader, I frequently need to blow off steam. You try being responsible for the health and happiness of 26 million people, all while battling South Korean capitalists and Yankee colonisers!

As a fun-loving millennial, my jolly image is important to me. It's helped win over masses of foreigners. They think: *A guy who's always grinning couldn't be evil, could he?* In addition, a lifetime of revelry has taught me everything there is to know about successful shindigs. As an ardent socialist, I believe in distributing resources equally, including knowledge. So this book is my gift to mankind, my attempt to save them from mediocre wingdings. Pretty

---

* Honestly, there's nothing funnier than a clown in fear of his life.

generous, eh? To think most of the planet believes I'm some homicidal maniac . . .

There are many such misconceptions about me and the nation I rule. You hear North Korea referred to as a 'hermit kingdom'. Tell me, would a hermit throw wild, all-night ragers? Also, the term 'rogue state' gets tossed about. I happen to think that sounds cool. A loveable rogue. Basically the Han Solo of states. And as for being part of an 'axis of evil'? Remember, the phrase was first used by George W. Bush, a harebrained cowpoke who wouldn't know his axis from his elbow. That dumbass only came to power because his daddy was president.

Seriously, I get such a bad rap it's unbelievable. People say I run a 'cult of personality'. Well, at least I have a personality! That's more than can be said for most Western leaders. Olaf Scholz? Keir Starmer? They wouldn't know a good time if it launched a ten-megaton warhead at their population centre. Me, I'm built different. I'm a bloody good laugh, always cracking jokes with my generals and beaming as we point at some test launch or military parade.

Furthermore, they call me a dictator. Um, have they seen the name of my country?

The *Democratic* People's **Republic** of Korea. Doesn't sound like a dictatorship to me. If my grandfather wanted the Undemocratic Tyrant's One-Party-State of Korea, he'd have called it that. In the end, these accusations can be traced back to one source: the US State Department. By the way, shout-out to the CIA analysts reading this to better understand my psychology. Sorry to disappoint you, but I don't have psychology: I'm a well-adjusted bloke who's not even slightly insane.

Oh, and while we're talking grievances, I'd like to address the nepo baby discourse. Some unkind souls have suggested that my success derives less from merit than from being the third generation of the all-powerful Kim dynasty. This could not be further from the truth. Yes, I'm part of the Mount Paektu bloodline, associated with Dangun, the human son of a god and a bear who founded the first Korean kingdom 4,000 years ago. But unlike Maude Apatow, Lily-Rose Depp or Blue Ivy Carter, I worked my magnificently proportioned arse off to get where I am. So no, I'm not a nepo baby. I hope the status of this book as masterpiece and international bestseller will finally put such allegations to rest.

Kim Jong FUN is designed to codify the best practices in party-planning. My grandfather invented Juche, or 'self-reliance', a distinctly Korean form of socialism based on independence from foreign interference. In the same vein, I will now outline the correct ideology for hosting a party. Naysayers might suggest my advice is only applicable to the scion of a hereditary dictatorship, making the book all but pointless. If they do suggest that, they'll be executed by anti-aircraft gun. Take that, naysayers!

No doubt Western propagandists will label me an out-of-touch hedonist, carousing while his failed state burns. However, I don't just throw parties for my own enjoyment. They're also for the people around me. Truth be told, North Korean life can be a little austere. Not for me, but for the man on the street, your Average Jong. These guys toil fourteen hours a day in the factory, then spend evenings at their local party chapter, receiving lessons on correct ideology. Such dedication to the revolution is commendable, but sometimes they need to let their hair down. (Not literally: we have very strict guidelines when it comes to hairstyle.)

Above all, parties are a chance for me to be among my people, lighting up lives and basking in adoration. Do they always make me happy? Of course not. I have my blue moments, like any other demi-god. Sometimes I question the applause that greets me at every turn. What if I'm not a world-historical genius, benevolent ruler and massively endowed playa pimp? What if my subjects only smile because they fear the re-education camp? What if everyone secretly hates me?

But no, that's silly. I'm amazing. Definitely. I assumed control of a nuclear power at the age of 27. How many men can say that? (Just me, I checked.) So yes, let's banish all thoughts of inadequacy and get ready to boogie down. Grab your handbag, your glad rags and your pack of counterfeit Marlboros. To paraphrase Western harlot Miley Cyrus, it's a party in the DPRK!

On-the-spot Guidance

As I travel the length and breadth of our glorious nation, from Hamhung to Manpo, I make a point of issuing 'on-the-spot guidance' to comrades I meet, telling engineers, doctors and nuclear physicists how to do their jobs. They're always loudly appreciative, so I hope to recreate the experience in sections like this. Think of them as golden nuggets of information, much like the Chicken McNuggets loved by Americans. While reactionary and subversive, those things are undeniably delicious. Actually, I might have my jet pick some up from Beijing . . .

KIM JONG UN IS THE HOST WITH THE MOST*!

* TACTICAL NUCLEAR WEAPONS

Acknowledgements

First off, I want to thank Kim Jong Un, AKA me. As with North Korea's thriving economy and triumphant development of the hydrogen bomb, I consider myself solely responsible for this book's excellence. I suggest that struggling Western writers such as Stephen King and J.K. Rowling study my command of prose and effortless marshalling of ideas.

I would also like to thank Jason Statham, whose cinematic oeuvre – from the *Transporter* series to *The Beekeeper* – means so much to me. In particular, his portrayal of Chev Chelios in both *Crank* and *Crank 2: High Voltage*, which always inspires me to be a better man.

Finally, I would like to thank Richard Madeley. He knows why.

Dedication

To my late father,
Eternal Leader Kim Jong Il,
and grandfather,
Eternal Leader and father of the nation
Kim Il Sung.

Also, to Scarlett Johansson.
Scarlett, come to Pyongyang!
You can stay at my place for free.

Denunciation

I would like to denounce the following enemies of the people:

Blithering codger Joe Biden.

Capitalist puppet Fumio Kishida.

Annoying Canadian Justin Trudeau.

Accursed scoundrel Choe Nam-gi, who is lower than a dog that all the other dogs beat up.

Hwang Yong-gon, who makes that dog look good by comparison.

And last but not least,
Richard Madeley, who I've gone off since I wrote the acknowledgements.

He knows what he did.

PART ONE: DILIGENT PREPARATION OF EXEMPLARY PARTY ACCORDING TO SOCIALIST PRINCIPLES

MARCHING DYNAMICALLY FORWARD TO A FUN TIME HAD BY ALL!

PRELIMINARIES

Sun Tzu is widely regarded as the greatest military strategist in history (after me). In his *Art of War*, he writes:

> The general who wins the battle makes many calculations in his temple before the battle is fought. The general who loses makes but few calculations beforehand.

This applies just as much to the art of partying (for 'general' read 'party host', and for 'battle' read 'mondo piss-up'). Dos are made or broken in the planning phase, so you should nail down as many aspects as possible. To quote both the Boy Scouts and Scar from *The Lion King*, be prepared. Let's start at the beginning . . .

Occasion

When, and for what reason, should you throw a party? If you're me, you've got plenty of stuff to commemorate. There's my birthday, as well as those of my dad (the Day of the Shining Star) and granddad (the Day of the Sun). There's Army Day and Party Foundation Day. Most importantly, there's the anniversary of North Korea's founding (9 September 1948). At seventy-five years, my country has existed longer than the Soviet Union. Suck it, Stalin!

That's not to mention my near-endless achievements, all of which merit celebration. These range from increased turnip yield to successful launches of intercontinental ballistic missiles. Of course, all North Korea's launches are successful. You may have read that our rockets keep plopping into the Sea of Japan, but these are the depraved lies of counter-revolutionaries and Western swine.

Another excuse for a party is me receiving a new title. Here are some that I plan to give myself in the coming months:

- Chief Grand Poobah
- Mack Daddy and Ten-inch Gangsta

- Most Excellent Player of Wordle
- King in the North (love *Game of Thrones*)
- Police Commissioner of the City of New York
- Lucasian Professor of Mathematics at Cambridge University
- Papa's Special Little Guy
- Pokémon League Champion (Sinnoh Region)
- Certified Lover Boy

At the end of the day, though, I don't need an excuse: if I want to party, I party. Otherwise, what's the point of having legions of servants? The only issue is when someone throws a rival party (by which I mean an event on the same

---

On-the-spot Guidance

Decadent US rappers the Beastly Boys once claimed 'you gotta fight . . . for your right . . . to paaaaarty'. This is despicable imperialist propaganda. North Koreans party as and when their leader commands. Further provocations from the Beastly Boys will be met with a terrible and overwhelming response.

That said, *License to Ill* slaps.

day). Such traitors can expect to be purged without remorse. This is a lesson I learned in my professional life: just because you're the best doesn't mean you should tolerate any competition whatsoever.

Guest List

What would a party be without guests? Pretty sick, actually. I could eat all the profiteroles and really let rip during karaoke. Nonetheless, it's traditional to get some bodies in the room. But which bodies? A smart host has strict criteria. Regarding potential guests, ask yourself the following questions:

1. Is it likely this person wants to kill me?
2. Am I planning to have this person killed in the near future?
3. Can this person help maintain my stranglehold on power?
4. Is this person cute? (Only applicable to girls.)

If your answers to the first three are no, no and yes, feel free to invite them. If your answer to four is also yes, definitely invite them.

Here are some North Korean luminaries who make the cut:

My generals
The lads. The homies. The Legend Squad. Get a few sojus* in us and we're unstoppable. You might think the senior military command of a highly belligerent country would be stern and humourless. Not these guys! They laugh uproariously at my every joke. When I make a point, they give themselves whiplash by nodding so hard. They may all be in their seventies and eighties, but each of them parties like a frat boy.

Why are my generals so old? you ask. Well, Confucius teaches us to respect one's elders. And I do. I respect them to the max. That said, if a geezer falls asleep mid-party, I'm drawing a cock and balls on his face with permanent marker.

Nuclear scientists
Obviously, no one wants to fill their party with Poindexters, nerdlingers and geekazoids. They're always getting their protractors out, snickering at in-jokes and acting weird around

---

* Korean rice wine, the only rice wine worth drinking.

honeys. But nukes are essential to national security (by which I mean the preservation of the Kim dynasty), so it's worth raising egghead morale. I invite the least off-putting bomb wonks on the understanding they stay in a corner and keep the science shit to themselves.

My little sister, Kim Yo Jong
Yo Jong's the most powerful woman in North Korea (and the second-most powerful person after me), so I kind of have to invite her. Which isn't ideal, given what a drag she is. She's always bothering me with affairs of state: ratify this, provide launch codes for that, blah, blah, blah. Lighten up, sis! Foreign intelligence agencies claim she's really the one in charge, the power behind the throne, running things day to day. This is, needless to say, horseshit. I have complete authority, even when I'm ten sojus deep.

That said, Yo Jong is quite intimidating, and I'll admit to being scared of her. I also accept that her cheekbones are more prominent than mine.

My loser bro, Kim Jong Chol
Mendacious opponents sometimes call me Kim Jong Il's 'failson'. This is ludicrous on its face:

I am a tactical mastermind and a golden god. Even if I weren't, I could never be more of a failson than my older brother. Jong Chol's not involved in politics or anything cool like that. He just leads a boring life in Pyongyang, playing guitar in a band and listening to Eric Clapton records. While I'm smiting the American aggressors, he's mastering the chords to 'Layla'!

I invite the guy to all my parties, partly out of pity, partly to make me look better in comparison. Actually, it might be good that Jong Chol has so little get-up-and-go. My half-brother Kim Jong-nam was ambitious and look what happened to him: assassinated in a Kuala Lumpur airport with VX nerve agent. We still have no idea who did it – none at all. His death was doubly tragic, coming only four years after the execution of my uncle Jang Song-thaek. Anyway, they're both dead as hell, so they don't make the list.

The other Kims Jong Un
There are always spots on the guest list for my team of Saddam Hussein-style lookalikes. In the event of an assassination attempt, these guys are the perfect decoy. They're also great

for pulling pranks and look amazing in a conga line. Chosen for their close resemblance to me, each of them undergoes extensive plastic surgery and a fast-food diet to complete the illusion.

Someone I'm *not* trying to invite is the ol' ball-and-chain, Ri Sol-ju. Look, I love the gal, but her job's raising our unconfirmed number of children. Plus, I don't want her waving the rolling pin when I get my flirt on.

That's the North Koreans taken care of. However, a Kim Jong Un party should be an international affair. Here are some foreign VIPs to spice things up . . .

Xi Jinping
This guy's basically my sugar daddy, so I have no choice but to invite him to parties. Fortunately, it's just a courtesy invite: Xi never shows. He's too busy trying to end democracy in Hong Kong and Taiwan. And you know what? I'm glad not to see him. I shouldn't vent, but I plain don't like the man. It's well

known he has little time for North Korea, and he always treats me like some barmy, irrelevant princeling. Can you imagine?

Dude thinks he's such a big-shot, just because he rules over 1.4 billion people. Yes, that's technically more than my 26 million subjects, but it's quality not quantity. The fact is North Korea's a thousand times cooler and more powerful than China, and I only invite Xi to my parties because I feel sorry for him. Also, if you want to wind the guy up, just mention his striking resemblance to Winnie the Pooh.

Vladimir Putin
Vladimir Vladimirovich is an utter drip with zero banter. Sad Vlad, I call him. Again, though, I'll sling an invite because there's no danger of him actually turning up. The guy's a total hypochondriac and a weirdo. Since the Western scam that is Covid, he's been afraid to travel, shake hands or take meetings at tables less than a kilometre long.

And it's not like he was a chill hang prior to 2020. Vlad's idea of a good time is getting shirtless and wrestling a Kamchatka brown bear. At least, that's according to his propagandists. Lord knows what he's really into.

Dennis Rodman

Now we're talking. This guy is the life and soul of any party. I first met Dennis 'The Worm' Rodman in 2013. The five-time NBA champ came to visit my Pyongyang pad, along with three of the Harlem Globetrotters and a bunch of *VICE* journalists. We shot a few hoops, had a few laughs and we've been thick as thieves ever since. One night, we got absolutely smashed on soju and Dennis gave a long, rambling toast, concluding, 'Marshal, your father and your grandfather did some fucked-up shit. But you, you're trying to make a change, and I love you for that.' I'd have had anyone else killed on the spot. From the Rodster, though, it was charming.

Some people wonder why the leader of an intensely conformist society would be friends with a guy known for wearing dresses, getting facial piercings and dying his hair pink. The answer? Because I say so. Dennis is the greatest rebounding forward in NBA history and – I'll admit it – my soulmate. Also, he's the perfect drill partner. I'm actually able to dunk on him, even though he's a foot taller than me.

NOTE ON LONELINESS

They say the loneliest place in the world is a crowded room. I disagree: an empty room is loneliest, because there's no one there to say how great you are. And I should know, having been intensely lonely as a boy. I always had extravagant luxuries – private cinema, pinball machines, Lego out the wazoo – but there were no other kids to play with. I've been told that growing up friendless and spoiled can cause psychological problems in later life. Fortunately, this wasn't the case with me. In fact, I was recently declared the sanest man in Korea.

Invitations

Persuading someone to attend your soiree is a fine art. Say I wanted to invite the forty-fifth (and possibly forty-seventh) President of the United States, Donald J. Trump. It would be necessary to entice the real-estate mogul with a thoughtful message. Sweet talk him, basically. After all, Mr Trump has high standards: he used to party with respected US financier Jeffrey Epstein. At the same time, I would need to bear in mind our own complex history.

My relationship with Trump got off to a rocky start. He engaged in some sabre-rattling, threatening me with 'fire and fury like the world has never seen'. To which I responded: 'I will surely and definitely tame the mentally deranged US dotard with fire.' You have to admit, that's a sick burn – we're talking Kendrick-level bars. But things greatly improved with our famous 2018 summit in Singapore.

To the astonishment of every nation, I met on equal terms with the so-called 'Leader of the Free World'. There was a dissonant moment at lunch, when Trump asked a photographer to make us look 'nice and handsome and thin'. Some interpreted that last adjective as a jibe at me. I didn't care. I had achieved a diplomatic coup of historic proportions. Also, for once, mine wasn't the most eccentric hairstyle in the room.

Since then, Trump and I have had an excellent working relationship. Here's how I might tailor an invite to good old Agent Orange.

Template #1:
Invitation for The Donald

Dear Esteemed US Warlord Trump,

Hail Visionary Leader, Gold-wigged Master of Lucre and Orange Sun of the American Empire! We in the Democratic* People's Republic continue to admire you with utmost fervency. You have dominion over the hoglike horde known as MAGA. You inspired an insurrection against the global hegemon on January 6. And you put your virility beyond all doubt by bedding cherished thespian Stormy Daniels. Incidentally, we were horrified to learn of your persecution by the corrupt US legal system. Since when was it a crime to give a beautiful woman the best night of her life?

With all that in mind, I – the prodigious Kim Jong Un – request the pleasure of your company. Every effort will be made to accommodate you. Food will be adapted to your Western palate (I have had our top scientists work around the clock to analyse and recreate the McDonald's Fillet-O-Fish). We will play your favourite heterosexual music, from Elton John's 'Tiny Dancer' to 'Macho Man' by the Village People. We may not have the calibre of celebrity guest to which you are accustomed – Jon Voight,

Kid Rock, etc. – but we will have such notable figures as General Kang Sun-nam and Vice Marshal Ri Yong-gil, along with your Celebrity Apprentice *co-star Dennis Rodman.*

So please do come. I would be honoured to put you up at my compound, which is often called the Mar-a-Lago of East Asia. When you're ready to go home, I'll have you escorted to Pyongyang International by a division of tanks. Nothing but the best for my bud!

Yours with yuge respect,

The equally virile Kim Jong Un

* Not Democratic like your rival, befuddled mummy Joe Biden.

When planning large gatherings, you needn't be so personal. If you're throwing open the Ryongsong Residence for an all-night rager, you're going to need hundreds of guests. Why not publicise the event on state TV? You could get that newsreader who always sounds like she's about to cry. Or you can distribute more general invites. For instance . . .

Template #2:
Invitation for Mass Circulation

Dear loyal servant of the righteous Kim dynasty,

You are hereby ordered to attend and have a great time at Kim Jong Un's party, which is to commemorate the overwhelming victory of North Korean forces at the Battle of Kaesong-Munsan. Please cancel any weddings, funerals or surgeries that might conflict with this event. Rejoice at the opportunity to breathe the same air as legendary paragon Kim Jong Un!

Anyone who leaves before midnight will be shipped to Pukchang Concentration Camp for re-education.

Yours imperiously,

Jongers

On-the-spot Guidance

Never mix up your list of invitations with your list of executions. I did this once and it made for a very awkward evening. Plus, a bunch of my friends got executed.

NOTE ON DINNER PARTIES

People sometimes imagine their dream dinner party, choosing guests from beyond the grave. What would it be like to break bread with the smartest and most significant humans of all time? For yours truly, it would be a snooze. I can't think of a single historical figure who has anything to teach me. Alexander the Great? I make him look like Alexander the Adequate. Confucius? I could pull the *Analects* out my arse. Albert Einstein? Hey, Al, here's a theory of relativity: my dad was Kim Jong Il and my granddad was Kim Il Sung, which means everything I say is right. Now comb your hair, put your tongue away and piss off back to the 40s.

No, I'm not interested in hanging out with old, dead men. Young, live women? That's more like it. My ideal dinner party would include the following females:

Scarlett Johansson
She could wear one of her iconic movie costumes, like – oh, I don't know – the skin-tight catsuit from *Iron Man 2*.

Sydney Sweeney

There's something about the *Euphoria* star I find compelling, though I can't put my finger on them. I just sense she'd be a committed and hard-working comrade.

Kim Kardashian

If she married me, she'd be Kim Kim. Pretty funny! Though I don't want to get on Kanye's bad side – that guy's crazy.

MAY OUR ENEMIES EXPERIENCE FOMO*!

* FEAR OF MASS OBLITERATION

SETTING

As a wise man – probably me – once said: location, location, location. Try as you might, you cannot throw a successful party in a void. I have a secret prison known as 'The Void', and there are no parties there, believe me. But I digress. You're going to need a venue, decorations for said venue and security for said decorated venue. 'Ooh, Marshal Kim,' I hear you cry, 'please go into more detail on the aforementioned points.' Well, shut up, because I'm about to do that.

Venue

As the unquestioned ruler of North Korea, I am able to choose from a range of exquisite locales. For instance, my main compound, which covers almost five square miles in north-east Pyongyang. Sometimes known as Central Luxury Mansion, it features an Olympic-size swimming pool complete with waterslide. Pool party, anyone? There's nothing I love more than executing a dive-bomb and then grabbing a margarita from the floating bar.

Alas, North Korean social mores are a check on poolside fun. Women wear conservative costumes, so there are no bikinied baddies to ogle. The only flesh on display is that of my ancient generals. And who wants to see saggy old man boobs or ball sacks flapping out of trunks? Still, at least I get a chance to show off my intimidating physique.

Other venues include my compound in Kangdong district, with its bowling alley, shooting range, horse stables, soccer field and race track, and my vast waterfront property at Wonsan, perfect for beach parties, barbecues and luaus. For an extra-large jamboree, I might select the Rungrado 1st of May Stadium, with its capacity of 114,000. Drastic measures are needed when you're as popular as I am.

Then there's the biggest venue of all: nature. As a rugged outdoorsman, I love partying *al fresco*. I especially like to take guests hunting with goshawks, the national bird of North Korea. Something appeals to me about watching a remorseless killer bear down on small creatures. If it rains, no matter. I just take it as an omen and have my advisers executed.

Decor

Communist architecture has an undeserved reputation for drabness. I can assure the reader, the grey brutalist blocks in which I reside are hella aesthetic, as stylish as they are bombproof. Still, when you're hosting, it never hurts to jazz up the place. Here are the best ways to pimp your compound:

Flags
You'll need both the *Ramhongsaek Konghwagukgi* ('blue-and-red-coloured flag of the republic') and the flag of the Workers' Party of Korea. If you have fewer than a dozen of each, this will be interpreted as political subversion through insufficient patriotism. Not having enough red flags is a real red flag.

Portraits
It's mandatory for North Koreans to hang a portrait of me in their home. Subjects can't go a day without seeing this lovely round face. Why should parties be any different? I'm

told my eyes follow you around the room. Sometimes literally, when they have miniature cameras built in.

Statues
Portraits are all well and good, but why stop at two dimensions? A solid-gold Kim Jong Un statue will zhuzh up any occasion. While there are statues of me outside every public building in North Korea, there's no harm in erecting a new one in the middle of your venue. Guests can congregate around it and have stimulating conversations about my lantern jaw and kind gaze.

Murals
These should be in the Socialist Realist style and depict me doing benevolent stuff. For instance . . .

- Handing out sweets and medication to a gang of cherubic kids.
- Saving a group of trapped miners by lifting a six-tonne boulder over my head.
- Kicking South Korean premier Yoon Suk Yeol in the nuts and making him go cross-eyed.
- Using the DeLorean from *Back to the Future*

to travel to the 30s and run over Emperor Hirohito.

Balloons

In the red, white and blue of the North Korean flag, naturally. A game I like to play involves filling the balloons with chlorine rather than helium. Then, if someone displeases me, I can throw a dart at the balloon nearest to them. It's, as they say, a real gas.

Flowers

Flower arrangements are ideal for concealing bugs. With these, you can monitor your guests' conversation for any trace of disloyalty. If they

---

On-the-spot Guidance

Consider the practical as well as the aesthetic. A good example is furniture placement. For some mysterious reason, I have a chronic problem with my ankles (our top medical personnel are baffled). Because of this, I make sure every party I host is replete with futons, beanbag chairs and fainting couches. Hammocks are also dope.

criticise Dear Leader, those flowers get reused at their funeral.

Security

One of the benefits of ruling a hyper-militarised surveillance state is that you have no shortage of bouncers. Just as North Korea exercises total control over its borders, nobody gets into a party without my say-so. Enforcing this is my security detail, the Supreme Guard Command. Think the US Secret Service, but way cooler and way manlier.

On-the-spot Guidance

A wise host knows that a party is never just a party: it can always be used for other purposes. For instance, to cover the sale of illegal arms. Parties are also a good place to have adversaries arrested and publicly humiliated, like I did with Uncle Jang at a meeting of the politburo. This has the added advantage of putting the fear of God in other guests.

Seriously, you will not believe how strong my bodyguards are. Each of them is more lethal than Bruce Lee, Jean-Claude Van Damme and Steven Seagal put together. If you so much as think of gatecrashing, guess what? You're already dead. These guys are the best of the best. And they need to be. Despite my universal popularity, I'm subject to assassination attempts every other week. For some reason, loads of people want to kill me.

Positions on my security detail are highly coveted and entry requirements are strict. To even be in with a chance, you must meet the following criteria:

- 6'2" minimum
- 8" minimum
- Male-model handsome
- Able to hold breath for over five minutes
- Able to carry me over shoulder (no small feat, given my muscle mass)
- Able to keep me company and talk basketball, chicks, etc.
- Willing to watch my favourite Scarlett Johansson films repeatedly (*Don Jon, Vicky Christina Barcelona, We Bought a Zoo*)

- Can run alongside my car, like Clint Eastwood in *In the Line of Fire*
- Can shoot an assassin who's holding Kim Basinger hostage, like Michael Douglas in *The Sentinel*
- Would take a bullet for me, like the bodyguard in *The Bodyguard*.

KILLJOYS WILL NOT BE TOLERATED! WE SHALL ACHIEVE FINAL VICTORY OVER PARTY POOPERS!

FASHION

Strong rulers are known for their iconic looks, from Stalin's walrus moustache to Mussolini's summer fez. If one wishes to inspire love and fear in one's subjects, dressing with swag is essential. This is equally true, if not truer, at a party. As host, you'll want to stand out, be the cynosure of all eyes, radiate flair and sophistication. Which is quite easy when every other guy's in uniform.

The Fit

Clothing is intensely personal, so all I can say is what works for me. Please take into account that I am likely hotter and in better shape than you. There are looks I can pull off that most men only dream of. Any attempt to approximate my drip is doomed to failure.

In public, my style's more Juche than Gucci. I keep things traditional – we're talking black

Mao suit with loose-fitting trousers and comfy leather shoes (to accommodate my gout). Call it communist chic. It's classic, elegant and doesn't at all make me look like a weirdo who just wandered out of the 50s. In private, though, I like to mix things up. Here are some of my favourite ensembles:

Island Style
As a rotund party animal, I naturally gravitate towards Hawaiian shirts. Not that I've ever been to Hawaii, a colony of the detested US empire. In any case, these shirts are fun, eye-catching and forgiving of my trademark girth. Not that it needs to be forgiven! I'm an advocate of body positivity (for me, not anyone else).

Pro tip: combine your Hawaiian shirt with shorts, sandals and a hollowed-out coconut with straw and miniature umbrella.

Soldier Style
I'm Commander-in-Chief of the Korean People's Army, so I like to – as American intellectual RuPaul might put it – serve military realness. I have a super-cute white uniform, featuring tassels, gold epaulettes and one of those

mushroom-shaped caps only worn by us. Very manly.

Complement this with a Type 88, the standard-issue rifle of the KPA, itself a North Korean improvement on the AK-74. Fatal and fierce!

Preppy Style
Think Ray-Bans, Ralph Lauren polo shirt, sweater worn over the shoulders. Carry a tennis racket for extra credibility. This is a good way to make people think you do sports, while avoiding the need to get sweaty and out of breath.

The Cut

Now your outfit's sorted, you need to make sure your hair's on fleek. My standard hairstyle – sharp fade, heavily waxed bouffant – is rightly iconic. But I'm not afraid to get nutty with it.

Here are some of the radically different styles I might pick for an occasion.

'The Boss'
Smart, authoritative, understated. This haircut says 'Relax, enjoy the party, but remember I could have your bloodline ended on a whim.'

'The Playboy'
Raffish. Debonaire. Full of *joie de vivre.* Men want to be him; women want to be with him. Deep down, though, this stud has a heart of gold.

'The Iconoclast'
Watch out for this guy. He's a groovy cat who lets his freak flag fly. He may be a consummate legislator and military tactician, but he also has an artistic side.

Accessories

Another way to make an impression is to accessorise. Sporting a vivid or unusual item – feather boa, Flavor Flav clock necklace, etc. – will garner lots of attention. In the Pick-up Artist community they call this 'peacocking'. Of course, I don't need to pick up women: every woman in North Korea (and, I presume, the world) wants me already. Still, I like to stand out.

North Koreans have to wear red pins with the faces of my dad and granddad. Fortunately, there are other accessories one can turn to. Such as . . .

1. A Giant Hat

I'm internationally known for my wide array of large hats. In winter, I'll don a fur one with a red star on it. In summer, I favour a wide-brimmed, Van Gogh-style straw hat. While touring a weapons factory, I might plump for a humble train driver's cap. Here's some of the headgear I bust out when I'm in party mode:

Fedoras
Perfect for tipping at a woman as you call her 'm'lady'. I'm told the fillies love and are charmed by this. For bonus points, follow up by saying, 'A libation, perchance?'

Victorian-style toppers
These enhance my already imposing height (five foot, seven inches). Plus, I can hide useful things under them (recording device, grenade, canister of phosphine gas, etc.).

Propeller beanies
These show guests you're a wacky, humorous guy. I've asked my scientists to build one that can actually take flight, in case of a palace coup. Prototypes aren't promising.

2. A Sick-ass Weapon

Up your cool quotient with a katana, blunderbuss or pair of gold-plated revolvers. No replicas, because where's the fun in that? If the party gets boring, you can always wave your sword around or fire your gun. Sick-ass weapons are a conversation starter (and, if needed, a conversation ender).

3. Medals

A fabulous accessory. North Korean generals wear row upon row of them (more than they could possibly earn), which means I have to up the ante. I like to wear all two hundred of mine at once, with medals covering my chest, spreading down my arms and legs, and even reaching my shoes. It looks rad, even though the weight is prohibitive. Also, if your party has a bouncy castle, the pointy ones might burst it. I know this from bitter experience.

What are all my medals for? you ask. Here's a (partial) list:

- Skeet shooting
- Launching satellites
- Animal husbandry
- 200-metre backstroke
- Penmanship
- Punctuality
- Advanced punctuality
- Being the best Kim Jong Un I can be
- Avoiding *Mandalorian* spoilers
- Watching things from a balcony

- Pointing approvingly at warheads
- Knowing all the lyrics to Eminem's 'Without Me'
- Podcast listening
- Completing *Sonic the Hedgehog 2* with all the chaos emeralds
- Drinking a pint of Guinness in one go
- Saving the Earth from extraterrestrial invasion*
- Knock-knock jokes
- Consolidating power through swift, brutal purges
- Gun kata, the martial art made famous by Christian Bale in *Equilibrium*

NOTE ON FEMALE MODESTY

The unassailable virtue of North Korean women is world-renowned. Accordingly, their party attire is demure and elegant: either the traditional *hanbok* or the sort of gown Westerners wore in the 50s, before

---

* I saw a star that looked funny and told my generals to shoot it.

they were totally debauched. Even at the most jumpin' party, our lady comrades know their duty is to the nation, rather than fashion. They dress in a manner befitting the mothers (or future mothers) of the Korean People's Army.

Contrast this with the blasted hellscape that is America. In the so-called 'Land of the Free', females are compelled to walk around in varying states of nakedness. Rich entertainers like Rihanna, Jennifer Lopez and Doja Cat can be seen strutting the red carpet with breasts and buttocks exposed. I know, because I've spent hundreds of hours studying the photos. As one of the few North Koreans with access to the internet, I pore over images of slashed, sheer and slit outfits. I do so in order to better understand the enemy. And, naturally, I feel disgusted.

Here are the ensembles that most offend my sense of propriety:

1. Kendall Jenner, 2019 Vanity Fair Oscar Party: the model, socialite and businesswoman turned heads with this daring and risqué look. We're talking plunging black halter dress with split

skirt and entirely cut-away sides. As a man of staunch values, I didn't like it. Not one bit.

2. Emily Ratajkowski, Met Gala 2024: EmRata really let herself down here. Her see-through gown from Atelier Versace left vanishingly little to the imagination. I imagined a bit, though, and I was appalled.

3. Megan Fox, 2021 MTV VMAs: oh dear, oh dear, oh dear. The *Transformers* star flaunted her curves in a salaciously sheer Mugler midi dress. I would hate to be Machine Gun Kelly and share a bed with this wanton.

It's a sad state of affairs, but all is not lost. If these beautiful but misguided women would simply defect, I could teach them decorum, one to one.

PART TWO: RUTHLESS ENFORCEMENT OF GUESTS' PLEASURE DURING FIRST-RATE PARTY

THE HOSTING SKILLS OF PRECIOUS SOVEREIGN KIM JONG UN ARE A BEACON TO EVERY NATION!

REFRESHMENTS

Unlike the prisoners in your gulags, you have to keep guests fed and watered. Providing delectable refreshments is a surefire crowd pleaser. Otherwise, you may find yourself with a revolt on your hands. Not that I know anything about that. You'll never see 'Kim Jong Un' and 'revolting' in the same sentence.

Food

When it comes to things to eat, you can't say fairer than food. Some of that stuff's tasty as hell. I've even been known to partake myself. I'm a trencherman, a gourmand and a gastronome, hence my extensive collection of chins. This appreciation for the finer things in life is what makes me an incomparable host. I understand the vital importance to a party of laying on a decent spread. You can't let people starve! I mean, I absolutely *can* do that. I just don't want it ruining my evening.

With party food, I like to keep things simple: lobster, grilled pheasant, shark-fin soup, steamed turtle, barbecued goat meat and caviar. You might think it's difficult to stage extravagant feasts in a country with chronic food shortages. Not for a baller like me. I get delicacies flown in from around the world: risotto from Italy, steaks from Argentina, Kentucky Fried Chicken from Kentucky. From the Japanese imperialists, I source the finest sushi: seabass, fatty tuna, lobster sashimi. Much as I hate our erstwhile oppressors, I admit their food is *oishi*. I'm also a fan of tentacle porn.

While my tastes are international, I never sleep on North Korean cuisine. What's a banquet without mandu, japchae and bibimbap? Best of all is Pyongyang naengmyeon, hand-pulled buckwheat noodles in cold broth, which I'm told is popular in the South as well. North Koreans should be applauded for their culinary skill and ingenuity. They're amazing cooks when they get the ingredients. Which is always! No supply-chain issues here!

Of course, you can't have a slap-up Korean meal without rice. All my rice is grown in a private paddy field on the West coast. Beautiful female workers handpick each grain, ensuring they are flawless and of equal size. It's a comfort to me that my carbs are exclusively handled by hotties. I would estimate I consume, on average, a kilo of white rice a day. Being a sagacious ruler is hungry work!

Then there's dessert. Something I like to do is have my chefs bake a cake with my face on it. What could be more appetising? Also, that means guests can't have any: it would

---

On-the-spot Guidance

Kim Jong Un's Kimpeccable Kimchi

Kimchi, a traditional side dish made of fermented vegetables, is a must at Korean meals. This recipe, handed down from my grandfather to my father to me, is tasty and oh-so-simple.

Step 1: Order a servant to fetch you kimchi.

Step 2: Enjoy!

be disrespectful to eat the Comrade-General's face.* All the more for me . . .

Okay, so you've chosen your dishes. How best to serve them? Buffets aren't an option for me – the poisoners would have a field day. Instead, my food and drink is brought over by latex-gloved attendants. I recommend this, even if you don't share my security concerns. After all, sharing is for losers: a host should have the most. So put slop out for your guests and eat from a heavily guarded private stash.

If, for whatever reason, I don't get enough sustenance at the party, my team of private chefs are on call 24/7. Each of them is honoured to provide my habitual 3am snack. And my 4am and 5am snacks. Running the most functional and efficient state on earth burns mucho calories! Foreign analysts suggest that the pressures of my job cause me to stress eat. Wrong! I am too blessed to be stressed.

Let me confront something head on: there are those who view my lifestyle as obscene, given the deprivation my people endure. Firstly, as I've said a million times, there is no rationing or malnutrition in North Korea. Secondly, the

---

* Both in icing form and in real life.

people would suffer infinitely more if their leader was hangry. So the woke virtue-signallers can wind their necks in. I have no reason to feel guilty as I chomp on a turkey leg and throw it over my shoulder, Henry VIII-style.

KIM JONG UN'S CHEESE CORNER

Of all the dairy products, none means as much to me as cheese. I developed a taste for Emmental during my schooldays in Switzerland, and this kicked off a lifelong love affair. As well as being mental for Emmental, I'm mad for Manchego, cuckoo for Comté and gonzo for Gorgonzola. I pack in the pecorino and get through more Wensleydale than Wallace and Gromit. Doctors warn my dairy habit is unsustainable. I say it's worth a few extra kilos and a bit of gout.

I've only had negative cheese experiences twice. A few years back, my private chef brought me a slab that was mouldy as shit. The guy explained it was French Roquefort, whose veins of blue mould give it a sharp tang. Well, I know an attempted poisoning when I see one. Needless to say, I had him executed and his body dumped in the woods. Who's mouldy now?

My other bad encounter was with American cheese, which comes in jaundiced rubber flaps designed to top some greasy burger. Such processed filth is symbolic of the dying empire roundly defeated by Kim Il Sung in 1953. American cheese is perhaps the worst thing the Yanks have ever created, along with Covid, crack cocaine and AIDs. I wouldn't feed it to my dogs. Partly because they're full of political prisoners. Kidding!

P.S. It's a source of profound regret to me that North Korea has yet to produce a world-class cheese. I've sunk millions of dollars of UN humanitarian aid into our Cheese Development Programme, but so far the results have been chalky and bland. Still, I'm confident that one day we'll invent a cheese to rival feta, provolone and Stinking Bishop. Some object to this use of relief funds, but I believe it's for the greater gouda.

NOTE ON FOOD TASTERS

You may think food tasters are the preserve of medieval kings. Not so: modern leaders often take the precaution, even ones as venerated as me. You never know when some traitor might toxify your victuals. I've been told that, due to my majestic BMI, I'm resistant to most poisons. Still, a whack of strychnine will spoil the most delicious repast, so I always keep a taster on deck.

It's not like I'm being paranoid: I've had a dozen food tasters die since I took office. It's always sad to lose an employee. Plus, watching them convulse on the ground, foam dribbling from their lips, puts you right off your vol-au-vents. Those interested in the job will need a sensitive palate and a comprehensive knowledge of human biology. Most importantly, they'll need to exercise portion control. A good food taster eats just enough to detect adulterants and not a morsel more. I don't want some peon sharing my grub.

Drink

The average man takes about ten days to die of thirst – don't ask me how I know that! Your party's unlikely to last more than twelve hours, so terminal dehydration shouldn't be an issue. Still, a good host ensures guests remain lubricated. Let's start with soft options. Tea and coffee are party essentials, but too much caffeine gives me palpitations. When I want to feel alert, I prefer a highly sugared juice: Ribena, Um Bongo, Sunny D. Then there's everyone's favourite non-alcoholic beverage, the noble soda.

Unfortunately, North Korea lacks any domestic soda brand.* That's not a problem for me, though, since I import gallon upon gallon of Sprite, Fanta and – above all – Coca-Cola. Coke may be a symbol of American capitalist hegemony, but damn if the stuff's not moreish. I heard a rumour that you can dissolve a tooth if you leave it in Coke overnight. I tried this

---

* It's strange how capitalism – an otherwise wicked and moribund system – seems uniquely adept at producing fizzy drinks. I've consulted Marx, but he's oddly quiet on the subject.

with a whole body, but the thing went nowhere, not even the teeth. Anyway, my current soda of choice is Diet Pepsi (I'm watching my figure).

What about the stronger stuff? I'm a model of self-control, but now and then I like to raise the alcohol content of my sacred Mount Paektu blood. This is just one of the ways in which Kim Jong Un is a man of the people. Koreans are notorious boozers: in the South, they down an average of fourteen shots of hard liquor a week. Naturally, we in the North are even bigger legends. Any drink they can binge, we can binge better.

Our go-to is soju. At around 20% ABV, it slips down easy, but gets you sloshed with a quickness. It's also clear and colourless, which comes in handy. Sometimes I'll pretend I'm drinking soju when I'm really on water. I make my generals match me shot for shot until they're totally obliterated. Then I monitor them for signs of disloyalty. One slip of the tongue and they face a brutal morning after. Believe me, you don't want to be in front of the firing squad with a hangover.

I also like to import upmarket brands: Belvedere vodka, Diplomático rum, Johnnie Walker Blue Label. The official government salary in North Korea is about four US dollars a month, so folks appreciate you buying the fancy stuff. That's a lesson I learned from my father: he was the world's biggest buyer of Hennessy Paradis cognac during the 90s famine, importing nearly a million dollars' worth per year. If you want to tackle mass starvation, you need to get a buzz on.

What, you ask, about beer? This may surprise our detractors, but North Korea excels at making it. State-owned Taedonggang is the most popular brand domestically. In 2000, my father bought a traditional English brewery – Ushers of Trowbridge – and had it disassembled and shipped to Pyongyang. Since then, we've been slinging suds like nobody's business. North Korean beer is dark, full-bodied, hoppy and delicious, unlike the watery piss they make down south. Hite? More like shite.

We also have a thriving microbrewery scene: our lagers and IPAs wouldn't be out of place in Shoreditch, East London, or New York's Bushwick. I know what you're thinking: is there a risk that North Korean craft beer could lead to North Korean hipsters? In my all-seeing wisdom, I have taken steps to ensure no hipster exists above the 38th parallel. Anyone found in possession of checked flannel shirts, beanie hats, moustache wax or ironic tattoos will be made an example of.

As may be expected, the South has sabotaged my anti-hipster measures, flooding the border with Neutral Milk Hotel CDs and fixed-gear bicycles. They will cease such provocations or be chastened with nuclear fire.

Tobacco

Ah, ciggies. Lovely, lovely tabs . . .

Anyone who knows me, knows I'm a heavy smoker (both in the sense that I smoke heavily and that I weigh 300 pounds). It's a habit I share with my father and his father before him. Smoking is huge in North Korea. Practically everyone does it,* despite a lack of decent fags. North Korea is one of the largest producers of counterfeit cigarettes in the world, and our real stuff is rough as hell. Not an issue for me, of course: I only smoke luxury Yves Saint

---

* Except for ladies. We encourage them to find more appropriate hobbies, like childbirth.

Laurents. I'm constantly blasting the things, which gives my teeth their alluring yellow patina.

I find massive nicotine addiction a great way to manage stress. I see no health drawbacks in my hundred-a-day habit, and my personal physician agrees. Indeed, he claims my lungs are now protected by a salubrious layer of tar. The vivifying effects of carbon monoxide allow me to accomplish feats of great fortitude, such as walking fifty steps before getting out of breath.

And I don't stop at cancer sticks: occasionally I'll break out the humidor and share cigars with my generals. Cubans are my favourite (we have no trade embargo, unlike the United Snakes of AmeriKKKa). I hear the CIA wanted to kill Castro with an exploding cigar, so I always make sure someone else takes the first few puffs. To date, only a couple have combusted, but you can never be too careful. When I'm feeling opulent, I go for a hookah pipe, like the Caterpillar in *Alice's Adventures in Wonderland*, or Baron Harkonnen, the hero of Frank Herbert's *Dune*.

One thing I would never smoke is marijuana. Drugs are highly illegal in North Korea, and zero leniency is afforded those who puff the magic dragon. Why would I blaze anyway? I'm already a chill, blissed-out sort of dude. Also, I don't want to get the munchies and mess up my figure.

NOTE ON PSYCHOLOGY

While I was at Swiss boarding school, I heard about a psychiatrist called Sigmund Freud. He argued there's this thing called oral fixation. People who have it are constantly stuffing their faces because they didn't get enough tit time as a baby. Ridiculous – the guy was clearly a pervert and a quack. More like Sick Man Fraud! Point is, my psyche is one hundred per cent healthy, and I'm not trying to fill some gaping mother. I mean void!

LET US REFILL THE PUNCH BOWL WITH PRIDE AND ONE-HEARTED UNITY!

ENTERTAINMENT

A party's nothing without razzmatazz, and the Kim dynasty knows all about that. My granddad mixed showbiz with show trials. My dad was a major cinephile who kidnapped a South Korean director to make the communist version of *Godzilla*. And the military parades I plan get the highest ratings on state TV. When hosting a party, you should emulate our flair for the dramatic. After all, you don't want your guests getting bored (yawning in Dear Leader's presence is an executable offence).

Music

When Westerners think of Korean music, their minds inevitably turn to K-Pop. This demonstrates woeful ignorance. K-Pop is degenerate filth that has no place above the border. Its electronic beats and suggestive lyrics reveal how thoroughly South Korea has been corrupted by capitalism. North Korean music is far superior: instead of bubblegum pop, we have long, patriotic marches. Why would anyone listen to Blackpink or BTS when they can enjoy bangers like 'The Supreme Leader Makes Wise Decisions For Our Well-being' and 'Productivity in Graphite Mining Remains Excellent'?

At a party, though, you want something modern and danceable. My favourite act is Pyongyang's own Moranbong Band, whose hits include 'Let's Study', 'Advancing in Socialism' and 'We Will Follow You Only'. More demure than their K-Pop equivalents (but twice as glamorous), they have a fresh sound that can best be described as 'apocalyptic disco'. Check them out on YouTube! Or its patriotic North Korean alternative, MeTube.

The Moranbongs are sometimes described as the North Korean Spice Girls, but that's an unfair comparison. None of them are posh – our society is classless – and they're certainly not scary. It's more like Patriotic Spice, Loyal Spice, Marching Towards Victory Spice. Also, these girls aren't just singers: they're instrumentalists, playing electric guitar, electric violin, drums and synthesiser. No wonder they're musically talented: they know one wrong note could send them to the gulag.

Look, I'll admit I'm not wholly immune to the charms of K-Pop. I've tapped my toe to Girls' Generation's 'Gee'. I've taken TikTok dance challenges from NewJeans. And my bedroom walls are covered in posters of the idols I stan: Hyuna, Jihyo, Lalisa Manobal. Also, I saw Red Velvet at a reciprocal cultural visit in Pyongyang. They favoured us with two of their hit songs, 'Red Flavor' and 'Bad Boy'. (I wanted them to perform 'Psycho', but my sister vetoed that.)

Live music is always a hit, especially when performed by the original artist. Want Dua Lipa to sing for your guests? Or Mariah Carey, or Shania Twain? Why not send elite members of the Reconnaissance General Bureau to kidnap them?* The Shanghaied chanteuse will be upset to begin with and reluctant to perform.

---

* Hands off Taylor Swift, though. No security service on earth could handle her fans.

However, if you're like me, you'll win her over with your charm and an offer of two million dollars.

When live isn't an option, recordings will do. Sometimes, a judiciously curated playlist is all you need to get people on the dance floor. Due to internet restrictions, North Koreans are unable to use Spotify. Fortunately, I have my own music app: Despotify. It only streams songs with a patriotic message, and there's a propaganda ad every ten seconds. No foreign music, natch: I don't want people getting corrupted by the West, with its Lizzos, its Snoop Doggs and its Charli XCX.[*]

If your party's struck by a power cut, never fear: there's always the accordion. North Koreans love squeezeboxes, also known as 'the people's instrument'. The Soviets brought them into the country, and they soon took off due to their volume and portability. An accordion can fill a room without amplification, or be taken into the fields for breaks during harvest. Me

---

[*] Not that I hate all Western music! For instance, I approve of any artist who shares my blessed family name: Kim Wilde, Lil Kim, Kim Petras. Also, I enjoy Elton John's 'Rocket Man', for obvious reasons.

> ### *On-the-spot Guidance*
>
> Power in Pyongyang goes out at 10pm, so make sure your party's done by then. This isn't a problem for me, of course: my palace has its own generators.

and my mates love to down a few sojus and go Weird Al mode.

And what's music without dancing? My standard move is the horse-riding dance from 'Pyongyang Style' (formerly known as 'Gangnam Style'). Some people say I look like Psy. I take exception to this: the man is a decadent cockroach. Unless he wants to defect, in which case all is forgiven. Jae-sang, come to Pyongyang! We could collab, or just bond over being chubby funsters.

Games

Being a military superpower, the DPRK places a high premium on physical fitness. Sport is hugely popular, allowing young people to express themselves in a society where self-expression is rare (for some reason). Friendly matches can be a fun addition to one's party, whether five-a-side soccer, netball or water polo. However, the best party sport is basketball.

As you may have guessed from my aforementioned Rodmania, I'm a lifelong b-ball nut. It was a waking dream to talk tactics with Dennis and to watch the Harlem Globetrotters – America's finest team – play an exhibition game. I would love to be visited one day by Michael Jordan, so I can give him on-the-spot guidance re: dribbling. Then I could show him my trick of jumping six feet in the air, rotating 1080 degrees and slam-dunking so hard it shatters the backboard.

On the less sporty, more ludic side, I'm keen on the following party games:

- **Human chess.** Does what it says on the tin. Thirty-two costumed participants move around a giant board as my competitor and I bellow instructions through a megaphone. As you might expect, I'm a chess grandmaster. I like to play a custom version based on my life (every piece is a pawn, and I win by default).

- **Race across the DMZ.** It's a minefield out there – literally! A fun and effective way to get rid of dissidents. The only winner is the guy watching through binoculars (me).

- **Smash the piñata.** But instead of candy, it contains a general who talked back. The idea is to get out my aggression – who needs therapy?

- **North Korean roulette.** A drinking game in which one of the shots is laced with VX nerve agent. I love this, but only as a spectator. It would be a major ball-ache if I died – months of the populace weeping, keening, rending their garments, etc.

Something I've intended to do for yonks is stage an actual *Squid Game.* You may be wondering how I know about the Netflix mega-hit: after all, North Koreans are forbidden to consume any media from the South. As ever, there's an exception in my case. I'm constantly binging K-dramas: *Alchemy of Souls*, *Perfect Marriage Revenge*, *Extraordinary Attorney Woo*. I do this to better understand how Western thought has pervaded South Korea. Also, the plot lines are kind of addictive. Will Naksu end up with Jang Uk?!

The upshot is, I loved 2021's *Squid Game*, in which desperate people risk their lives for a prize of 45.6 billion won. I'm told it's an allegory for the brutalising nature of free market capitalism. My main takeaway was how dope it would be if that happened IRL. Of course, my *Squid Game* wouldn't be an exact recreation of the show. I don't need 455 peasants to die horribly. I'd settle for 300 maimed. Also, on Netflix, the games are held to amuse wealthy sadists with a psychopathic disregard for the less fortunate. In this case, they'd be held for me, a loveable scamp.

Spectacle

If there's one thing a totalitarian regime loves, it's pageantry. You have millions at your beck and call, so why not stage something memorable for your guests? I'm always partial to a military parade or a flypast of the mighty North Korean air force – all three planes. But my favourite is the Arirang Mass Games, in which 30,000 well-trained schoolchildren hold up cards to form images of my face. Totalitarian? More like 'totally rad'!

Conventional hosts might consider a fireworks display. Bor-ing! Instead of Roman candles and Catherine wheels, why not test-launch a missile over the Sea of Japan? Not only will the crowd *ooh* and *ahh*, it serves as a warning to imperialist pig-dogs (I'm looking at you, America). Delight for my guests and terror for my enemies: that's the difference at a Kim party.

Failing that, I'm more than willing to step in and entertain with displays of my physical prowess. Government materials distributed to every North Korean describe me as proficient in horseback archery, Krav Maga and extreme pogo. While I can't recall ever doing those things, it's safe to assume I am.

NOTE ON LIVE COMEDY

I love a laugh, me. In fact, I'm famed for the G-ness of my SOH. You can't spell 'Kim Jong Un' without 'joking' (or 'nuking', but that's another story). Predictably, then, I'm a big fan of stand-up. I love all kinds of comedian, from stars like Dave Chappelle and Bill Burr to less mainstream acts like Daniel Kitson and Stewart Lee. I even commissioned a replica of the red leather suit from Eddie Murphy's *Delirious*, though I haven't debuted it in public.

Hiring a stand-up for your party is a high-risk, high-reward strategy. If you find the right performer to amuse your guests, vibes will be off the charts. Fortunately, there are many acts to choose from when you're loaded. Guys like Jimmy Carr and Michael McIntyre are constantly chasing corporate gigs. Reach out to their representatives. If they're happy to perform for banks and oil companies, they shouldn't object to a guy who's been repeatedly sanctioned by the UN Security Council.

That said, I'd suggest hiring a local comedian, one who can weave in material about the area. My go-to guy is Pak In-dok, 'the Jerry Seinfeld of North Korea'. These are a couple of jests from his latest performance:

> *What's the deal with our great nation's mineral exports? Thanks to the ceaseless brilliance of the Generalissimo, zinc production reached 30 thousand tonnes in 2021!*

And . . .

The only thing greater than Comrade Kim Jong Un's love of the people is his tremendous physical attractiveness. To look upon his form is to behold a thousand golden suns!

I'll admit these gags are a bit close to the bone. Still, I can take them on the chin. Just another of my wonderful qualities.

OUR SKILL AT KARAOKE TERRIFIES THE AMERICAN ENEMY!

BONUS:
KIM'S FILM RECOMMENDATIONS

As mentioned, my dad was a fiend for the silver screen. In this respect, as in all respects, I am carrying on his immortal legacy. By watching thousands of DVDs and VHSs, I have cultivated faultless taste in movies. I judge each of them on two metrics: a) do they convey proper Juche messages, ennobling the worker's heart? And b) do they feature hot women? Here are my findings:

Approved Movies

Gladiator (2000)
This Oscar-winning epic has much to teach us about self-sacrifice and martial valour. Naturally, I relate hard to Russell Crowe's Maximus Decimus Meridius. Like the Roman general, I'm solely motivated by honour and love of country. Of course, I'm nothing like

Joaquin Phoenix's Commodus, a lunatic nepo baby who murders family members.

Despicable Me (2010)
I may be an iron-willed commander of unconquerable mettle, but I'm not made of stone. I happily admit that Minions are as cute as they are hilarious. They love ba-na-na! Superb. Also, as a guy with millions of fanatical followers, I can relate to the protagonist, Gru. Not that I'm some kind of cartoon villain.

Furthermore, *Despicable Me* carries important socialist messages. The Minions evince laudable solidarity when they pool their resources and enable their master to steal the moon. The sequel, *Despicable Me 2*, is a similarly rich text. El Macho turning the Minions into purple monsters with PX-41 mutagen reflects how Western propaganda turns a loyal populace against their own interests. This is a sobering reminder from beloved French humorist Pierre Coffin.

Cats (2019)
No morals to glean from this one: it's just a bloody good film. I've watched it over forty times, and it always leaves me in tears. Seeing Jason Derulo inhabit Rum Tum

Tugger makes one glad the Lumière brothers created filmmaking. And the inclusion of comedic geniuses Rebel Wilson and James Corden as Jennyanydots and Bustopher Jones respectively? Icing on the cake.

Banned Movies

Team America: World Police (2004)
The creators of *South Park* were way out of line with this puppet-based calumny. It depicts my father as a cackling supervillain in ludicrous granny glasses. Eventually, he's revealed to be a giant extraterrestrial cockroach. Why would anyone satirise Kim Jong Il, who was a saint and not at all risible? The film should have stuck to mocking someone genuinely dangerous: Alec Baldwin.

Despite this vicious and unprovoked attack, I remain a huge *South Park* fan. Sure, Matt and Trey dishonoured my father, but they also invented Cartman and Mr Hanky the Christmas Poo, so I can't stay cross.

Red Dawn (2012)
This film stars Thor and features North Korea invading the United States to free its people

from their corporate overlords. So far, so good: that's something we could and should do. But the movie takes a dismaying turn when a group of hot young Americans start fighting back. By the time credits roll, the Yankees have inflicted crushing defeats upon their North Korean occupiers. Totally unrealistic: zero stars.

The Interview (2014)

Hoo boy. Look, I have no objection to films being made about me. In fact, I think I should be the subject of every film. This one, however, takes the biscuit and shoves the biscuit into its anus. It stars chortling stoners Seth Rogen and James Franco as the lowest of the low: American journalists. Joining them is traitor-to-the-Korean-peninsula Randall Park, who plays a grotesque parody of yours truly. The film is vulgar and slanderous, and shows my fiery death in explicit detail. Worst of all, it depicts me as a sadistic man-child obsessed with Katy Perry's 'Firework'. That is a complete misrepresentation. My favourite Katy Perry song is 'California Gurls'.

Needless to say, this travesty was met with a devastating reprisal. The studio behind *The Interview*, Sony Pictures, found themselves the subject of a huge cyberattack on 24 November 2014. A hacker group linked with North Korea, Guardians of Peace, leaked 100 terabytes of their private data. This included first-draft scripts, unreleased movies, executive salaries and embarrassing email exchanges. For instance, it was revealed the producer Scott Rudin had called Angelina Jolie 'a minimally talented spoiled brat'. Harsh! I'm just glad no one thinks that of me.

So, yes, those are my movie thoughts. I'm sure you'll agree I make Martin Scorsese and Mark Kermode look like neophytes. In addition to being a hardcore cineaste, I'm also a fan of prestige TV. My favourite recent show is HBO's *Succession*. It's about a dynasty whose members scheme and stab each other in the back to achieve power. I do love a bit of escapism. People recommend *Game of Thrones*, but that's too close to home.

RULES

The key to a happy, prosperous country is having endless rules. Parties are no different. Everybody likes fun, but you can't let your shindig get out of hand. That means laying down the law up front.

Here are my cardinal party rules (to be enforced by the Ministry of State Security):

1. All toasts must be dedicated, explicitly and exclusively, to the glory of Chairman Kim Jong Un.

2. Laughing at the Supreme Leader's jokes is mandatory, and failure to do so will result in several years' hard labour. This is also the case if laughter is insufficiently forceful or convincing.

3. Those leaving the party early (or, as I call them, 'defectors') will be picked off by sniper fire.

4. No one is to hook up without the express permission of Kim Jong Un, son of Eternal General Secretary Kim Jong Il, grandson of Eternal President Kim Il Sung.

5. No double-dipping. That's just gross.

Each of these cardinal rules carries the death penalty. In addition, I have hundreds of lesser rules (which also carry the death penalty). Many of them are contradictory, and they can be revised at any time. By me. In my head. Don't bother complaining if you get caught out: ignorance of the law is no excuse.

FORBIDDEN KIM JONG UN NICKNAMES

For the avoidance of doubt, here are some names you are <u>not</u> allowed to call me:

- The Buffoon with the Bouffant
- Kim Not-Nice-But-Dim
- Plus-size Stalin
- Edam Hussein
- Fatilla the Hun
- Pol Pot Pie

- The Weight Dictator
- The Great Inflator
- Pussolini
- Shitler

Hopefully this puts an end to these insults and doesn't just teach them to more people.

P.S. You may have noticed this preamble is quite a bit longer than the others. That's because rules – and my subjects' total adherence to them – are so important. They're the difference between a thriving North Korea and some kind of dystopian hellhole.

Etiquette*

Etiquette is the code of polite behaviour within a specific social circle. Points of etiquette aren't as serious as rules – they're more a

---

* I considered making this section a multiple-choice questionnaire. Then I remembered that in North Korea there is only one choice: obey the regime.

guide to best practice. Unless, of course, you're interacting with me, in which case faux pas can be fatal. Here are some dos and don'ts when it comes to socialising with the Supreme Leader:

DO applaud everything I do. Insufficient vigour is punishable by death. Genuinely: in my uncle Jang's trial, 'half-hearted clapping' was cited as evidence. There's always a reason to convict of treason!

DON'T turn your back on me. All I ask is the same consideration shown to Queen Elizabeth II. Unless, of course, you're a lady with junk in her trunk. Nicki Minaj or Megan Thee Stallion can turn their backs on me any time . . .

DO address me as 'Marshal', 'General-Comrade' or another of my sundry titles. After a few shots of soju, I might say, 'Hey, call me Jong Un.' This is a test. If you drop the formality, you're gulag-bound.

DON'T hold drinks in your right hand. If I receive a moist, sticky handshake, I'm going to assume it's a bioweapon.

DO keep your conversation light. Avoid controversial subjects, like food scarcity or the country's GDP. Or anything that might discomfort me in any way. Often, I'll issue guests a list of approved topics (my skill at *Call of Duty*, the sweetness of my breath, etc.).

DON'T bring anyone who wasn't invited. Security is paramount, and every guest must pass multiple layers of screening. If I see an unfamiliar face, that face becomes unfamiliar to its owner.

Of course, faux pas go both ways. I've been known, every now and then, to put my gout-

---

On-the-spot Guidance

In her hit 2009 single 'TiK ToK', the singer Ke$ha – an American so decadent she has money in her name – states 'the party don't start till I walk in'. This is literally true if you're Kim Jong Un. Due to my intense fear of missing out, it's verboten to enjoy things when I'm not around.

ridden foot in it. What happens if I forget someone's name, or bring up a relative of theirs I had executed? In such instances, my interlocutor should apologise for making me feel awkward. If I really get embarrassed, I can have them exiled to remote, mountainous Ryanggang Province. Problem solved!

Drugs

Everybody knows drugs and parties don't mix. No one has ever sparked a doobie, popped a pill or snorted a fat rail and gone on to have a good night. It's just as well, then, that drugs are totally illegal in North Korea. North Koreans don't need cannabis or molly to induce euphoria. They already get that from their devotion to me. For this reason, the peninsula's upper half is a drug-free zone.

So-called Western journalists claim otherwise. They say the DPRK makes more meth than Walter White, and that 'ice' is widely used throughout the country. This is patently absurd. People take drugs to escape a painful or depressing reality. Why would anyone in North Korea want to escape? To quote a song our children are made to sing, 'We Have Nothing to Envy in This World'.*

Despite being above the law, I don't partake in illicit substances. The only drugs I need are nicotine, alcohol and cheese. That said, I did once OD on Camembert. I started with Cheddar, a classic gateway cheese, before moving to the hard stuff (Gruyère). Soon I was battling full-blown cheese addiction. Through staggering willpower, I managed to overcome it, and now I only eat cheese five times a day. Point is, I'd never sully this body with drugs.

It's very common in the West for high-powered individuals to abuse stimulants, but I'm not tempted by that filth. I already have inexhaustible energy and immense powers of concentration. How else could I write this entire book in one sitting?

---

* I've actually written a song of my own, a charity single along the lines of 'Do They Know It's Christmas?' It's called 'Do They Know It's Day of the Foundation of the Republic?' The song invites North Koreans to sympathise with the less fortunate (those who aren't ruled by Kim Jong Un).

Health and Safety

Anyone casually acquainted with North Korea knows how much I value my people's welfare. This boundless compassion informs my hosting style. I always want my guests to make it home in one piece (unless I deliberately had them divided). I therefore take extraordinary measures to make sure my parties are a safe space. Of course, since 2020, social events have been haunted by the spectre of Covid.

At the height of the pandemic, gatherings were banned across the world. Fortunately, due to my perspicacious leadership, there was no Partygate in Pyongyang. To date, North Korea has had zero cases of Covid, with my decisive action stopping the virus in its tracks. Due to unyielding projection of strength, virions were too afraid to cross the border. The World Health Organisation claims this isn't true, but they are reactionary agents of global capital.

Drawing on my deep knowledge of epidemiology, I identified all possible disease vectors. For instance, I worried troops in the Joint Security Area might get infected by their southern counterparts. To stop this happening, I came up with a simple, cost-effective solution:

every morning, our boys would wrap themselves in clingfilm from head to toe. I'm told this was a tremendous success, barring a few suffocations.

My other big Covid idea was to put a moat of hand sanitiser around my compound and make visitors swim across it. This didn't come to pass due to logistical issues (I forget what those were). Fortunately, I'm not a Putin-style hypochondriac. I'm confident my anatomy can handle anything coronavirus throws at it. The only social distancing I do is when I send mates to the gulag.

Not that I play fast and loose when it comes to hygiene. For example, I have a dedicated toilet-seat tester, Mr Yang. Every time I need to poop (or feel like peeing sitting down), Yang places his butt on the seat to check it's not coated with VX or sarin. This has the added advantage of warming said item up. I'm also hyper-vigilant against ailments that affect my capacity to govern. During flu season, I expect my bodyguards to identify and shoot down any germ particle that flies near me.

PART THREE: FURTHER INSIGHTS FROM REMARKABLE GENIUS KIM JONG UN

PARTY LIKE IT'S 1948*!

* THE YEAR THE GREATEST COUNTRY ON EARTH WAS FOUNDED

SOCIAL TIPS

Picture the scene: your party is in full swing. The drinks are flowing, the guests are mingling, the Minister for State Security has replaced his dress cap with a lampshade (hilarious). You are king of the world, the host of hosts. But then, finding yourself surrounded by an expectant crowd, you open your mouth to speak and nothing comes out. You, the indomitable Kim Jong Un, are tongue-tied. Your cheeks burn bright and sweat pools upon your forehead. This is as mortifying as those dreams you keep having, the ones where you turn up at school, only to realise you're naked and your penis has transformed into a field mouse. It scurries away and is snatched up by a swooping goshawk.

    What's the lesson here? That social skills are an essential part of a host's arsenal. You can organise the best party in the world,* but if you behave like a wallflower freakazoid no one

---

* I frequently do!

will have fun. It is therefore imperative that you master the bonhomie and self-assurance needed to put your guests at ease. I'm an adept socialiser, as you can see from the copious news footage in which I hug and kiss smaller children, make grizzled veterans howl with laughter and leave old ladies weeping with joy. People love my company! Unless they're just pretending. But why would they do that?

Overcoming Anxiety

You may find it hard to believe, but I often suffer from shyness and imposter syndrome. These are lingering effects of a solitary boyhood, most of which I spent alone in my father's compound, playing *Super Mario* on the Nintendo 64. My only friends were the eponymous Italian plumber, along with Princess Peach, Yoshi and, to a lesser extent, Bowser. I wanted *GoldenEye*, but Dad thought playing from the perspective of a decadent Western spy might corrupt me.

For the longest time, I found social engagements unbearably awkward. Fortunately, I was able to turn things round, and now

I'm the life and soul of every party. A gay gadabout.* A walking dispenser of social lubricant. How did I achieve this? Largely through iron will that you, dear reader, have no hope of replicating. But I also used certain techniques you can emulate.

When in need of a confidence boost, try repeating a mantra. I often say the following:

- You are loveable, you are capable, you have nukes.

- If you end the world, it was meant to happen.

- You are not a sucka MC. In fact, you're the Kim Jong Illest.

- Putin, Xi and Assad aren't laughing behind your back.

- The amount you masturbate, and what you watch while doing it, is normal.

At the same time, you should be countering negative thoughts. Here's some examples of how to do so:

---

* No homo.

Negative Thought: Everyone remembers the failure of your latest missile test.

Counter: In the words of Wayne Gretzky – or possibly me – 'You miss one hundred per cent of the shots you don't take.'

Negative Thought: Your wife is spending a lot of time with her bodyguard, who's jacked and looks like Jin from BTS.

Counter: You're an Adonis and more than any woman could want. Plus, Beom-seok isn't *that* jacked.

Negative Thought: You're not a god amongst men, you're a scared little boy. Your power is an accident of birth. You're just the weirdo son of a weirdo son. It's a sick joke that a clown like you controls millions of lives.

Counter: Shut up. SHUT UP SHUT UP SHUT UP!

Remember, these thoughts are paranoid nonsense. They can – and should – be disregarded entirely. There's no way you could become a better person, or improve the lives of those around you, by engaging with them.

Anxiety can be particularly bad when you have to make a speech, as I'm invariably called upon to do at parties. A common piece of advice to public speakers is to imagine their audience naked. I'm not a fan of this technique, given most people around me are octogenarian top brass. All those wrinkled old-guy dicks would put me off my crudités. Believe me: I once ordered the generals to strip as a prank. Anyway, to calm myself down, I imagine I could have anyone in my audience executed. Which has the advantage of being true!

   If all else fails, a foolproof way to deal with social anxiety is to get totally wasted on soju. Alcohol furnishes you with the demented self-belief an autocrat needs. You'll fancy yourself a Wildean wit, a Baryshnikov-level dancer and intensely desirable to ladies and gentlemen alike. Some inhibitions may remain, but no one can tell you're blushing when you're red-faced already.

   Still, excessive drinking can be risky when you're an absolute monarch. Not to your health – that divine liver can take a battering – but to those around you. What if you wake up the next day with a blinding hangover, only to discover you ordered everyone called Ri be

On-the-spot Guidance

Everyone agrees I'm an orator equal to Pericles, Martin Luther King Jr and Kim Jong Il. Here are my tips for a crowd-pleasing speech:

- Mention all the cool shit you're getting done: record grain production, a push towards afforestation and water conservation, the hundred-foot statue of Optimus Prime in Kim Il Sung Square, etc.

- Give plenty of shout-outs. Just be aware the recipient might assume they're being denounced as a counter-revolutionary. Put them at ease right off the bat: 'General O Kyong-thaek in the hizzouse! General O's a bloody good bloke and I do not suspect him of treason . . . currently.'

- Keep things lighthearted. If your party is taking place during a particularly vicious purge, maybe say something like: 'It's great to see so many friendly faces – I thought I'd signed some of your death warrants!'

executed? Or sent dozens of anthrax balloons over the DMZ? Or launched an ICBM directly at Washington? You probably meant those commands as a funny joke, but your generals aren't fluent in sarcasm. Plus, it would be a death sentence for them to question or disobey you. Now the world's ending and you haven't even had a chance to down some Berocca and order an Egg McMuffin.

Fortunately, that kind of thing has only happened to me a couple of times. I've since reined in my boozing.

NOTE ON ICEBREAKERS

For reasons I don't fully understand, people are often nervous when meeting me. That's where icebreakers come in. Breaking the ice* means doing or saying something to put your interlocutor at ease and facilitate the flow of conversation. My preferred technique is self-deprecating humour. For instance, I might make a joke about my weight.

---

* Not to be confused with the activity I make prisoners do in winter.

However, this creates a catch-22. If my listener laughs, they acknowledge I'm fat and get sent to the gulag. If they don't, they suggest I'm unfunny and get sent to the gulag.

Another method is silly humour. For example, inhaling helium from a party balloon and talking in a high-pitched, squeaky voice. Problem is, you might need to issue directives before the helium wears off. It's hard to sell the command 'fire the Hwasong-17' when you sound like Mickey Mouse. A non-gas-based alternative is celebrity impressions. I can do Morrissey, Gollum from *Lord of the Rings* and General O Kyong-thaek (not many people know him, but it's spot on).

Finally, you can break the ice with a conversation starter. Popular ones include 'What would be your perfect weekend?' and 'Have you done anything exciting lately?' A question I like is 'Who's your favourite world leader?' Of course, there's a correct answer. And if my conversation partner gets it wrong, they're going somewhere that rhymes with 'schmulag'.

Flirting

Let's be real: the main reason people go to parties – apart from seeing me – is to meet that special comrade. For the Korean Casanova, here are some state-approved pick-up lines:

- 'Did you expose me to chlorine gas? Cos you just took my breath away!'

- 'Did it hurt? When you fell from the peak of sacred Mount Paektu?'

- 'If being cute was a crime, I'd punish you and three generations of your family.'

- 'Are you Huichon Hydroelectric Power Station? Because you light up my life. Also, reports that you fail to generate power at full capacity are Western propaganda.'

- 'Are you the aim of our nuclear programme? Because you're da bomb.'

- 'I want you to be an object buried in the DMZ: mine.'

- 'I haven't experienced this much chemistry since I worked in a sarin plant.'

- 'I love Kim Jong Un above all, but you could come second.'

- 'Let us have healthy sons who lay down their lives to defend the fatherland!'

- 'I should call you *kimchi jeon*, cos, girl, you're looking like a snack.'

Actually, forget I said all that. It's probably best if no one flirts except Kim 'Rizz Lord' Jong Un. In North Korea, singles aren't motivated by such base things as sex and romance. Instead, they bond over mutual love of the revolution. This is how it should be: I am completely opposed to women having casual intercourse. Unless it's with me. Then it's their patriotic duty . . .

Just kidding! I'm married – to the glamorous and beautiful Ri Sol-ju – so things never go beyond flirting. Though if I did fool around, there isn't much she could do about it. Sorry, Sol-ju – that's what you get for choosing a bad boy!

Defusing Fights

Like Sparta or the Mongol Empire before it, the DPRK is a fierce martial society. When you combine that with soju and my tendency to set underlings against each other, donnybrooks are inevitable. Say two of your generals get in a shouting match over who has more respect for your inspired management of the nuclear weapons programme. They start shoving each other, but kind of in slow motion because they're so old. How do you lower the temperature and avert senile violence?

As a tender, loving ruler, I would get between them and announce something along these lines:

'Friends! Friends! In the name of Marshal Kim Jong Un, cease this fracas! Can't you see you're on the same side? It doesn't matter who loves me most. What matters is you both love me more than friends, family and life itself. Now, why don't we mosey on down to the bar and grab ourselves some daiquiris?'

Your elderly generals will pause and then hug each other tightly. There will be a flood of tears and apologies. At this point, you should motion to your guards to take both of them away. If they really respected your inspired management of the nuclear weapons programme, they wouldn't have backed down.*

Fights between women are even more unseemly and must be suppressed with alacrity. Unless the women resolve their differences by wrestling in a pool of jelly while wearing bikinis. Before anyone says that's sexist, bear in mind I extended conscription to North Korean women in 2015. This proves I'm a feminist ally and a woke bae. Sisters are doin' it for themselves!†

---

* My ability to pacify coots has come in handy when dealing with such superannuated leaders as Ayatollah Khamenei and Joe Biden. Sling them a Werther's Original and they'll do whatever you say.
† By 'doin' it' I mean 'pledging to die for the glorious Kim dynasty'.

LET US PARTY ACCORDING TO THE DECISIONS OF THE FOURTH PLENARY MEETING OF THE EIGHTH CENTRAL COMMITTEE OF THE WORKERS' PARTY OF KOREA!

AFTERMATH

Your shindig's a wrap. *C'est finis*. The fat lady has sung (figuratively speaking – all the ladies who sing at my parties are in great shape). But just because the guests have passed out or staggered off doesn't mean your work is done. Like the leader of a much-maligned socialist republic, a host's duties never end. Here's how to ace the morning after . . .

The Clean-up

Wild bacchanals create detritus: smashed vases, spilled drinks, vomit. Plus, I've heard there's such a thing as party poopers. Disgusting. So, who's going to handle the mess? Certainly not me: I've never cleaned or tidied in my life. I'm the leader of an egalitarian society, not some pathetic drudge. Fortunately, the Ryongsong Residence is full of skivvies, all desperate to clear up after me. If they're shorthanded, my secret police can always help. They have lots of experience making things disappear and forensically scrubbing a scene.

Let's talk about the elephant in the room. Not literally: I've only had a pachyderm at one of my parties (he went on a rampage and had to be tranquillised). No, I'm talking about dead guests. It's an unhappy subject, but, as Confucius said, shit happens. Maybe someone falls down a flight of stairs. Or chokes on a shrimp tartlet. Or shoots themselves ten times in the back of the head. Now you've got a body on your hands. What do you do?

A classic move is to have the offending cadaver buried in your backyard. My backyard is huge, so I don't have to worry about running out of room. I could bury hundreds of bodies without making a dent. Hypothetically, I mean. Plus it's great for the begonias. Another method is to have the stiff weighed down with stones and dumped in the Daedong River. This carries some risk, theoretically, as police trawl and dredge such bodies of water. But then the police are controlled by the Ministry of Social Security, which answers to the State Affairs Commission, whose president is . . . guess who?

Finally, if you're a fastidious sort, you might want to have your boys use industrial chemicals. These turn the carcass into a sort of human soup, easily flushed away. No need for bone saws or anything like that. Remember, if you're liquefying a corpse with hydrofluoric acid, do so in a polyethylene tub: it will dissolve any other container and then you'll have a real mess on your hands. (I'm basing this on that one episode of *Breaking Bad*, and certainly not on my own experience.)

Settling Scores

Revenge is a dish best served cold – and in a doggy bag. Once your party's been and gone, you'll want to deal with guests who P-ed you O. Here are some behaviours I consider worthy of retribution:

- Making a joke or reference I don't get.
- Taking the last Monster Munch, even though Flamin' Hot is famously my favourite.
- Implying that our country's generation of fissile material is anything less than miraculous.

- Mentioning Luke Skywalker's cameo in the *Mandalorian* Season Two finale, when I haven't had a chance to watch it yet.
- Beating me at musical chairs. Or pin the tail on the donkey. Or anything.

Such gross offences inevitably provoke a righteous rage. What should one do with it? My advice is to never bear grudges against the living. This leaves you two options: either let go of your anger, or make sure the person who angered you stops living. If I'm honest, I find the latter more satisfying.

When settling scores, my actions are swift and merciless. Indefinite detention, summary execution, the sky's the limit. It doesn't matter if you're one of my closest confidantes – irk me in any way and you're shit out of luck. That's life: one day you're part of the squad, the next you're in front of the firing squad.

Handling Embarrassment

The only thing worse than waking up with a hangover is waking up with a hangover and the knowledge you disgraced yourself last night. Say you got a bit too merry and vomited on your Finance Minister's wife. Or drove a T-34 tank through the ballroom. Or climbed on a table, pulled out your dick and waved it about, screaming 'I'm Kim Dong Un'. (These are definitely one hundred per cent made-up examples.) How do you live it down?

The main thing to remember is that you are a ruthless autocrat, so your underlings would be foolhardy to gossip. Still, you may want to purge them for your own peace of mind. Maybe General Jang Su-il won't tell anyone he saw you kissing a King Charles spaniel. But why take the chance? Have him sent to the countryside and the hound quietly disposed of. Alas, this may not be enough.

You can banish as many people as you want, but you can't banish yourself. You'll still remember the Bad Thing. I myself have little capacity for shame – just as well, given my immiseration of the people, my regime's attitude to human rights, blah de blah. Even so, certain images play in my head on a torturous, never-ending loop. I've enquired about the 'neuralyzer' from *Men in Black*, a device that violent actor Will Smith uses to erase people's memory.

> ### *On-the-spot Guidance*
>
> Always carry a notepad to record any slights, micro-aggressions or weird vibes on the part of your guests. Then, the following day, you can pass their names to the secret police. Let the liquidations begin!

My spies tell me it's not real, but that's bullshit – I saw it in the film.

If you do find yourself in a shame spiral, remember this: other people are ants, and you are a god on earth. Everything you do is right, by virtue of your having done it. If you peed in the punch bowl, that must have been a good call.

BONUS: STATE-SANCTIONED LIMERICKS* TO BE RECITED AT PARTY

Our leader, the great Kim Jong Un,
Makes everyone dance to his tune.
The fools in the West
That we so detest
Will soon be sent off to the moon.

Jong Un is an autocrat who
Does things that a man ought to do:
This unflinching hunk'll
Bump off his uncle
And poison his half-brother too.

There once was a man from Pyongyang
Who from the most blessed loins sprang.
His dad, Kim Jong Il,
Passed on that strong will,
As well as a ginormous wang.

---

* Translator's note: these were tough to adapt from the original Korean.

Our Kim Jong Un's power is mega;
Belief his robustness does beggar.
The fact is, Kim Jong
Un is so strong,
He'd devastate Conor McGregor.

America's future is grim,
For Yanks are tremendously dim.
Had we grown up there,
That dimness we'd share
And call Kim Jong Un 'Jong Un Kim'.

With nukes – in the view of this rhymer –
The Marshal is no pantomimer.
Make fun of his girth
And he'll burn the whole Earth
Like that shot in the film *Oppenheimer*.

I feel for our dear Comrade Kim:
His foes spread such lies about him!
They call him a glutton
Who might push the button
And end the whole world on a whim!

SMITE SUBPAR CATERERS WITHOUT MERCY!

MEMORIES

Attending my party will invariably be the high point of a guest's life. Their graduation, their wedding day, the birth of their first child – all pale in comparison to briefly meeting my gaze as Tinie Tempah's 'Pass Out' blares in the background. They'll want reminders of this special night, which gives me a chance to seize the narrative. 'Who controls the past controls the future. Who controls the present controls the past.' That's a quote from *1984*, George Orwell's novel about a chill society that's fun to live in.

In most of the world, social media is a problem for hosts. Any guest can share proof that your bash was garish, depressing and poorly attended. Not so in the DPRK, where all social media is banned. You may not agree with my other laws, but you've got to admit I nailed that one. North Koreans don't get their brains warped by TikTok, Instagram or X-formerly-known-as-Twitter. This frees up their brains to be warped by me. Win–win!

In the absence of dissenting voices, how can one shape perceptions of one's party? Read on, dear reader . . .

Party Favours

These are small gifts, given to guests as a memento. They often come in pretty gift bags, festooned with ribbons. I like handing out favours with a North Korean twist. For instance:

- A handful of rice. Most North Koreans have to survive on a substitute made of dried corn kernels, so this is very thoughtful.
- A fresh portrait of yours truly to hang on the wall. Better keep it dusted, though! Otherwise it's gulag time.
- A novelty T-shirt with something funny on it. Something like 'once you go Kim, you never go slim', or 'I attended Kim Jong Un's party and all I got was this magnificent T-shirt'.
- Condoms with my face on the packet. Y'know, to get people in the mood. We could call them

'rubber Jongies'. Actually, scratch that: we need more soldiers in the Korean People's Army, so no protected sex.

You can also tailor gifts to a specific guest. For instance:

- An album of grainy images taken with a telephoto lens. These show your guest at home, walking to work, having illicit meetings, etc. You can include inscriptions, e.g. 'always watching over you – KJU'.
- A bullet with their name carved on it. Just to remind them of what's in store for anyone whose loyalty wavers.
- A powerful nerve agent concealed in a can of deodorant, alongside a fake Brazilian passport and the address of a high-profile defector.

Photos and Videos

In addition to my social-media policy (no social media), guests are not allowed to bring smartphones. The only cameras permitted belong to official state photographers, trained to shoot me in a way that accentuates my jawline. All photos from the party will be stored in the national archive, so guests subsequently denounced as traitors can be airbrushed out. If a guest is taller than me (unlikely – I'm 5'7"), they are required to kneel in photos. Otherwise, they will be taken by the security service and forcibly shortened.

As well as cameramen, I employ an official videographer to capture the mirth and merriment. This guy's a genius: he makes the most lacklustre party look like *Euphoria*. Plus, he adds these cool effects in post: star wipes, colour filters, CGI. One time he had me float in midair, shooting lasers from my hands. The footage is then edited into a montage to be shown on state TV. Under these images plays 'Friendly Father', a belter of a song that declares 'let's sing about Kim Jong Un, our great leader'. Seriously, check it out on YouTube – the thing slaps hard.

Press Coverage

In ex-imperial shithole Britain, the people are kept docile by publications like *Hello!* and *OK!* These placate the unwashed masses with details of glamorous celebrity parties. In North Korea, I am the ultimate celebrity: David Beckham, Harry Styles and Cara Delevingne all rolled into one. It makes sense, then, that North Koreans want to read about my fantastic functions.

The DPRK has no glossy magazines. What it does have is *Rodong Sinmun*, the government's official newspaper. A few years back, I suggested/ordered they start a society page to apprise the rank and file of my dos. Call it a totalitarian *Tatler*. The *Sinmun* boys write up events, praising each aspect with frantic hyperbole. Then I go over their panegyric to make sure it's fawning enough. Here's a recent account:

RYONGSONG DISTRICT, PYONGYANG

– Yesterday, the people's hearts were even gladder than usual. ~~Resplendent~~ Guardian of *Godlike* the Revolution Kim Jong Un threw a party that will assuredly enter the annals of history. All Koreans must celebrate this proud soiree, at which good vibes reigned supreme and innumerable shapes were thrown.

Displaying the same monolithic determination that causes the Americans to quake in their boots, Kim Jong Un steadfastly planned and executed a party in honour of his new high score on Fruit Ninja. Thus he proved once again that he is the sole steward of our national destiny. The Kims will rule this country for all eternity, the immovable linchpin of Korean existence!

When two hundred guests arrived at the Ryongsong Residence, they were instantly bowled over by the Comrade-General's largesse. Buffet tables heaved with ham sandwiches and cheese-and-pineapple hedgehogs. On stands dotted around the venue were pointy, rainbow-coloured hats, party blowers and, of course, a tonne of (poppers.) The lofty love Kim Jong Un bears

Maybe 'party poppers'? I've heard it can mean something else in the West . . .

for his people could be discerned in every detail.

At 7 on the dot, our dashing host and his lovely lady wife appeared atop the central staircase. First Lady Ri sported a tasteful green dress and pearl brooch. Imperishable Marshal Kim – a person born of heaven – wore his much-mimicked black Kim suit. They descended into the crowd, kicking off an evening of ebullience and camaraderie and fun. On a raised platform, the tribute act Fatboy Kim performed North Korea-themed covers of 'Praise You' and 'Right Here, Right Now'.

There was only one sour moment, which – it goes without saying – had nothing to do with Kim's actions. At around 9.30, partygoers became aware of a loud popping sound. Comrade Kim, whose knowledge of military technology is unrivalled, immediately identified shots from a Tokarev TT-33 handgun.

'Assassin!' he cried in a deep and manly voice, pointing in the sound's direction. The heroes of the Supreme Guard Command responded by unleashing a volley of bullets. Fifteen guests were killed immediately.

After some investigation, it was determined that the source of the noise was someone pulling a party popper. While this may seem an innocent activity, pulling poppers without express permission is a subversive act. It's therefore just as well that Kim, in his wisdom, had the culprit shot. And a bunch of other people. In the end, responsibility lies with the waves of foreign assassins that make vigilance necessary.

Such unpleasantness was regrettable, but the remaining revellers soon got over it. Among them was General Jang Su-il, who told us, through patriotic tears: 'These festivities defy human understanding. If the Americans were to witness such proof of Comrade Kim's organisational ability, they would surrender immediately. I particularly enjoyed the olives stuffed with pimento.'

Outside the venue, Han Mun-gyu, of Pyongyang District 7, said: 'I was not invited to the Revered Comrade's party, which would have been far more than I deserve. But the knowledge that he was boogying down made my ~~gruel~~ sirloin steak taste all the sweeter. By the way, do you know if they had any food left over?'

margin notes:
- Maybe lose this whole section? Does it make me seem dumb?
- Maybe take him out of this? I might gulag the guy

How blessed are we, the Leader's beloved children, to exist in a time of such parties! He is truly our people's glory, a genius among geniuses! We vow with bleeding tears to call Kim Jong Un our supreme commander!

A decent start. Could we make it more fawning? - KJU

NOTE ON THANK-YOU LETTERS

These are obligatory. Any guest who doesn't furnish a grovelling message of gratitude will be declared an enemy of the people. Here's a template for you to work from:

Dear Potent/Acute/Justly Idolised Marshal Kim,

A million thanks for inviting me – a mere peasant – to your gorgeous/splendiferous/era-defining party. The ambience was agreeable/electrifying/off the chain, and the hors d'oeuvres were delicious/toothsome/succulent/ambrosial/peng. That popcorn chicken? Oof, madone!

Every Korean has cause to worship the name of Kim. Your grandfather defeated the Americans in the Fatherland Liberation War. Your father steered us through the Arduous March of the 90s. And now you have perfected the art of party-planning. Thank you, Beloved Leader. Thank you, thank you, thank you.

Yours abjectly/unworthily/punily,

Some Guy

CONCLUSION

Well, there you go. I, Brilliant Comrade Kim Jong Un, have penned another tome. And, like every challenge to which I turn my delicate but powerful hand, I absolutely smashed it. What will I do next? Reunite the Koreas under my rule? Travel to the bottom of the ocean, James Cameron style, and see the fucked-up fish? Build an escalator to the moon? These are all highly likely.

So, yeah, congrats to me on writing a book. And congrats to you on finishing it! You are now ready to graduate Kim Jong Un-iversity. Of course, you'll return to this work time and again. It contains more wisdom than can be absorbed in a single read. Or, indeed, the lifespan of a normal human. Perhaps, in millennia to come, our descendants will fully appreciate the text. Perhaps it's too monumental. Either way, please give it a five-star review on Amazon!

Have I learned anything by setting down party advice? Only that hosting has made me a better leader and leading has made me a better host. Like a leader, the party-planner must impose his* will upon countless underlings. Like a leader, the party-planner must anticipate problems and ruthlessly extirpate them. And like a leader, the party-planner must remember to have fun himself. Otherwise, why bother?

Fun is what I'm all about (hence the title of this book). Even my haters have to admit I seem like a laugh. It doesn't matter how many relatives I kill, or how much I oppress, brainwash and starve my captive population. It doesn't matter that I hold a quarter of a million political prisoners in the most abject conditions, or that I could bring about nuclear apocalypse on a whim. When you think of me, you see a round, ruddy face grinning broadly. Who could stay mad at that?

So I plan to have fun in perpetuity. I'm going to live it up until my soul leaves this

---

* I'd say 'his or her', but, as far as I'm aware, there are no female party-planners. The job's too important to be left up to dames.

body, travels to the summit of Mount Paektu and ascends to paradise. There I will find my father and grandfather, revelling among the clouds. They will smile, raise their shots of soju and toast me with a hearty *geonbae!*

This is Partymeister Kim Jong Un signing off.

Gamsahabnida!

LET'S ENSURE THE TIMELY PRODUCTION OF THE MATERIALS AND EQUIPMENT NECESSARY FOR AN EPIC NIGHT!

BONUS:
EXCELLENT MOVIE SCRIPT
BY KIM JONG UN

To my long list of accomplishments, one can now add 'screenwriter'. I know, I know: I'm a Stephen Fry-level polymath. If there were any more strings to my bow, the arrow wouldn't fit.

My most recent effort is a pulse-pounding action thriller, starring me as the sexy hero. I share it out of generosity to the Korean people (and desire to increase the word count).

MISSION KIM-POSSIBLE: PYONGYANG PROTOCOL

A Kim Jong Un Production

Written and Directed by
Kim Jong Un

Edited, Produced and Executive Produced by
Kim Jong Un

Starring

Kim Jong Un
as himself

with

Dwayne 'The Rock' Johnson
as Donald Trump

Scarlett Johansson
as Beautiful Lady Agent
in Love with Kim Jong Un

and

That Girl from *Squid Game*
as Kim Yo Jong

INT. PERSONAL GYM - DAY

A shirtless KIM JONG UN is midway through his daily work out. He's doing a barbell bench press, lifting an insane number of plates. His best friend, DONALD TRUMP, is spotting him.

          KIM JONG UN
One hundred and ninety-nine . . . Two hundred . . . Donny, can we add more weights?

          TRUMP
Sorry, boss, that's all one thousand pounds.

Kim sets down the barbell, gets to his feet and starts doing star jumps. Trump regards Kim's ripped physique with envy.

          TRUMP
I wish I was in such awe-inspiring shape. Too many American hamburgers, I'm afraid.

Kim spins and karate-chops a breeze block in half. He then pulls off a series of backflips at Olympic gold-medal standard. As we marvel at his washboard abs, his sister, KIM YO JONG, enters.

            KIM YO JONG
Good workout, brother?

            KIM JONG UN
Intense. I almost broke a sweat . . .

            KIM YO JONG
Well, your amazing physical talents are needed in the real world. I have a mission for you.

CUT TO:

EXT. BEACH – DAY

Kim Jong Un pilots a speedboat, flanked by a pair of mamacitas. He's wearing 18K-gold Ray-Ban aviators

*and looks unspeakably cool. This is
irrelevant to the plot.*

CUT TO:

INT. BRIEFING ROOM - DAY

*The Kim siblings stand in a high-tech
office in downtown Pyongyang. A large
screen shows Kim Jong Un's file, which
states he's killed the most men and
slept with the most chicks in the
history of spying.*

          KIM YO JONG

As I was saying, I have a mission for
you, Agent Leader.

*The screen shows a group of ugly,
barbaric AMERICAN MERCENARIES.*

          KIM YO JONG

Mumbling senex Joe Biden has sent a
team of operatives across the border.
Their goal? To spread misinformation
among the people.

                KIM JONG UN
Misinformation?

                KIM YO JONG
You know, that they're poor, hungry and have no human rights. That sort of thing.

                KIM JONG UN
How did mercenaries get through our defences?

                KIM YO JONG
They surfed ashore in the dead of night.

                KIM JONG UN
You mean like James Bond at the start of *Die Another Day*?

                KIM YO JONG
Exactly. Anyhoo, we need you to take these guys out.

                KIM JONG UN
Isn't that more properly a job for the Reconnaissance General Bureau?

                    KIM YO JONG
                      (nods)
Our agents are the finest and most
courageous in the world. Still, none
of them is as lethal or sexy as you.

                    KIM JONG UN
You make a compelling point, sister.
I shall go out in the field.

EXT. THE FIELD - DAY

Kim Jong Un walks through an actual field with his sidekick Donald Trump. Both wear leather trench coats and reflective shades.

                    KIM JONG UN
Stay frosty, T-Dog.

A COWARDLY AMERICAN ASSASSIN pops out of a bush and throws a knife at beloved leader Kim Jong Un. Seeing this, Trump hurls himself in front of the Comrade-General. He falls to the ground, knife embedded in his heart.

A pointless sacrifice - Kim would have easily caught the weapon. Still, it's sweet Trump loves him so much.

Demonstrating lightning-fast reflexes, Kim pulls twin Uzis from his coat and leaps sideways. He fires as he sails through the air in slow motion. The assassin is riddled with bullet holes and dies like a bitch.

Kim lands, rolls, and rises to his feet with the grace of a ballerina. But a manly one. A ballerino. He blows the smoke from his Uzi barrels and makes a clever quip.

          KIM JONG UN
Uzi come, Uzi go.

Kim kneels beside his mortally wounded pal. Trump coughs up a tonne of gross blood.

            TRUMP
Tell Ivanka and Barron I love them. Eric and Don Jr, not so much.

                    KIM JONG UN
Tell them yourself. You're gonna make
it.

                    TRUMP
We both know that's not true. You
have more understanding of anatomy
than any doctor.

                    KIM JONG UN
Yeah, I was just trying to be nice.
You're screwed. Sorry.

                    TRUMP
It's an honour to die for you, Dear
Leader. If I am to be remembered, let
it be as your less cool friend.

*Trump dies and voids his bowels
explosively, his digestive system
ravaged by a lifetime of fast food.*

                    KIM JONG UN
Goodnight, sweet prince. So passes
the only good American.

He leaves his buddy to lie there,

wisely concluding that the stench will prevent wild animals from eating his corpse.

CUT TO:

EXT. SKYSCRAPER - DAY

Now we're on a Pyongyang rooftop. Panoramic views of the glimmering metropolis. Kim Jong Un uses taekwondo (in which he's a 9th dan black belt) to fight a series of American mercenaries. He resembles a mix of John Wick, Neo from The Matrix, and real-life Keanu Reeves. He's demolishing the best fighters the US has, and it's not even difficult.

Soon only a couple of Biden's fiercest warriors are left. Wetting his pants, AMERICAN 1 turns to AMERICAN 2.

AMERICAN 1
Why did Comrade-General Kim efficaciously pursue a nuclear weapons

programme? Surely his fists are deterrent enough!

Kim Jong Un appears beside them and does a roundhouse kick that takes their heads clean off. He strikes a tight-as-fuck kung fu pose.

> KIM JONG UN
> Your move, Uncle Sam.

An APACHE HELICOPTER flies up, firing at Kim with its chain gun. He simply punches each bullet aside. Then he jumps fifty feet and kicks the tail of the helicopter, causing it to spin out of control. The shoddily manufactured US vehicle hits an adjacent building and EXPLODES in a multi-million-dollar pyrotechnic display. (There is no one inside the building because Kim, with preternatural foresight, had it evacuated earlier.)

A BEAUTIFUL LADY AGENT comes up behind Kim and puts a chrome-plated

Desert Eagle to his temple. She's a Scarlett Johansson type (by which I mean Scarlett Johansson). Before she can pull the trigger, she falls madly in love with him.

   BEAUTIFUL LADY AGENT
Fearless ruler Kim Jong Un, the American pigs sent me to kill you. However, I now realise you are the lodestar of the twenty-first century and the handsomest man I have ever seen.

She throws the gun away and falls to her knees.

  BEAUTIFUL LADY AGENT (CONT.)
Please grant me the honour of a swift execution.

Kim Jong Un gallantly helps ScarJo to her feet.

     KIM JONG UN
That won't be necessary. Kim Jong Un is merciful as well as handsome.

I have no desire to execute a defenceless woman.

He raises a flirtatious eyebrow.

          KIM JONG UN (CONT.)
Especially if she's hot.

Kim Jong Un and Beautiful Lady Agent kiss for five minutes.

          BEAUTIFUL LADY AGENT
A great warrior and a great lover? You're one hell of a man, Mr Kim.

          KIM JONG UN
Please, call me Respected Comrade.

They kiss for another five minutes. THE PEOPLE come up behind them.

          THE PEOPLE
Thank you, Supreme Leader, for protecting our beloved homeland on this and every day. Now, could you please keep frenching ScarJo, that

we may learn valuable lessons in lipsmanship?

                KIM JONG UN
The things I do for my subjects . . .

As he resumes canoodling with the husky-voiced starlet, and maybe even touches her butt, we FADE TO BLACK.

THE END

BUT KIM JONG UN WILL RETURN

IN

FROM PYONGYANG WITH LOVE

It's clear this work of genius can't be improved upon. All that's left is to get it made. But who has the vision to direct? Spielberg? Nolan? Villeneuve? My father's dream was to become a Hollywood filmmaker. Perhaps I shall direct it in his honour.

Anyway, *Mission Kim-possible: Pyongyang Protocol* is a guaranteed blockbuster. We're talking critical acclaim and boffo B.O. I predict my film will receive multiple Oscars, despite the unfair US sanctions against me. Best Screenplay is pretty much a lock. Or maybe Best Adapted Screenplay, given it's based on real events. I just hope ScarJo's at the ceremony . . .

DANCE LIKE COMRADE KIM JONG UN IS WATCHING! BECAUSE HE IS!

Supplementary Dedication

To the boys who dream of being dictators.

I believe in you.

Unless you're North Korean.

Then you should back off.

끝